THE TOP 10 WAYS TO RUIN THE FIRST DAY OF SCHOOL

THE TOP 10 WAYS TO RUIN THE FIRST DAY OF SCHOOL

Originally published as
The Top 10 Ways to Ruin the First Day of 5th Grade

KEN DERBY

SCHOLASTIC INC.

New York Toronto London Auckland Sydney
Mexico City New Delhi Hong Kong Buenos Aires

ACKNOWLEDGMENTS

I would like to thank Chris Crutcher for encouraging me
to "go for it" while this story was in its early stages;
Laura Backes for her advice and support;
Suzanne Reinoehl for pulling more "story" out of me
with her amazing editorial skill and instincts; Regina Griffin
for believing in Tony Baloney . . . and in me; John and
Kate Briggs for graciously "adopting" me into the Holiday
House family; George Nicholson and Paul Rodeen for their
enthusiastic representation; and to David Letterman for having
the best show on television for over a decade.

ISBN 0-439-80627-5

Originally published as *The Top 10 Ways to Ruin
the First Day of 5th Grade*
Copyright © 2004 by Kenneth Derby.
All rights reserved.
Published by Scholastic Inc.,
557 Broadway, New York, NY 10012,
by arrangement with Holiday House, Inc.
SCHOLASTIC and associated logos
are trademarks and/or registered trademarks
of Scholastic Inc.

12 11 10 9 8 7 6 5 4 3   6 7 8 9 10/0

Printed in the U.S.A.   40

First Scholastic printing, October 2005

THIS IS FOR MY SON TONY,
THE REAL "TONY BALONEY"

IN MEMORY
OF "ROCKETMAN"

CONTENTS

THE TOP 10 WAYS TO RUIN THE FIRST DAY OF SCHOOL

1.
Stupid Human Tricks

Tony Baloney stuck his head out of the fifth-grade boys' rest room and whispered, "Psst, Mo. Over here."

Mohammad bin Abdul Hamad bin Jamaluddin bin al-Rashid looked up from the drinking fountain. He had chocolate skin, puppy-dog eyes, and shiny black hair. Everybody called him Mo—for obvious reasons.

"What do you want?" Mo whispered.

"I want to show you something."

"Aw, come on, TB. We're supposed to be in class," Mo said.

Tony's real name was Anthony Madison. His mom always made him peanut butter and baloney sandwiches for lunch. He wouldn't eat anything else. Some kids called him Tony Baloney. Other kids called him TB for short.

Tony gave Mo his I-can't-believe-you're-going-to-wimp-out-on-me look.

"It'll only take a minute," said Tony.

"Mr. Gore's going to kill us," said Mo.

"He'll never find out. Come on."

Mo looked up and down the hallway. Not a soul was in sight. He went into the rest room.

"We shouldn't be doing this," Mo said. "It's the first day of school."

"You worry too much," said Tony. He faced the wall, climbed up on a toilet, and stood on the edge of the open bowl with his feet spread apart. Then he pulled a jump rope out of his back pocket.

"What are you going to do with that?" asked Mo.

"I'm going to flush and jump," Tony proudly said. "Nobody's ever jumped rope on an open flushing toilet before!"

"That's stupid," said Mo.

"Exactly," said Tony.

"I don't get it," said Mo.

"Stupid human tricks," said Tony.

"What?" asked Mo.

"You know. Like on the *Late Show with David Letterman*. Sometimes Dave invites people on his show to do stupid human tricks."

The *Late Show with David Letterman* was Tony's favorite television show. He loved staying up late on Friday nights to watch David Letterman interview famous guests. He loved the top ten lists (such as Top Ten Signs Your Kid Watches Too Much TV), the jokes, and the silly skits that David Letterman featured night after night.

"So," said Mo.

"So," Tony continued, "someday I'm going to flush and jump on the *Late Show*."

"Yeah, right," said Mo. "Hurry up."

Tony flushed the toilet and then swung the rope over his head. His first jump was perfect. His feet landed squarely on the seat of the toilet.

Jumps number two and three were pretty good.

Jump number four was not. At the last moment he'd looked up, turned his head, and said, "Cool, huh?"

His right foot missed the seat and plunged into the toilet.

"Way to go, TB," said Mo, clapping his hands.

Tony dropped the jump rope. "Mo?"

"What?"

"My foot is stuck," Tony said. "Mr. Gore is going to kill us."

"Great," said Mo as he grabbed Tony's leg. "Flush the toilet and I'll pull at the same time."

Tony flushed and Mo pulled. Nothing happened.

Tony flushed and Mo pulled again. Nothing happened—except that water filled the toilet and spilled onto the floor.

"We're dead now," said Mo.

"Yes, you are," said a voice behind them. "Exactly what's going on here, Mr. Madison and Mr. al-Rashid?"

Tony looked over his shoulder. Mr. Gore stood with his arms crossed over his huge chest. He wasn't happy.

Some kids called him Mr. Gorilla behind his back. That was understandable because he kind of looked like one. Everybody called him Mr. G to his face—unless they were brainless.

It wasn't good to make your fifth-grade teacher mad on the first day of school. It was even worse to make a former linebacker for the University of Missouri football team mad on the first day of school.

"What is going on here?" Mr. Gore repeated.

"Uh, stupid human tricks," said Tony.

"More like stupid Anthony tricks," said Mr. Gore. "Now get out of the toilet and get back to class."

"Can't," Tony said. "My foot's stuck."

Mr. Gore rolled his eyes and walked over to Tony. "On the count of three, wriggle your foot. I'll pull," Mr. Gore announced. "One, two, three!"

Mr. Gore leaned back and yanked as hard as he could. His feet shot out from under him, and he landed with a thud on the wet floor.

"I should have stayed with football," Mr. Gore grunted as he propped himself up on one elbow. "It was a lot safer."

"Uh, Mr. G. My foot's still stuck," said Tony.

Mr. Gore stood up. Water dripped from his clothes. "Tony, I think I'll leave you here for the rest of your life."

"Wow! I'd probably make the *Guinness Book of World Records*," said Tony, grinning weakly. "I'd be known as TTK—Tony the Toilet King. I'd be famous!"

"This is going to be a long year." Mr. Gore shook his head. "Mo, go and get help."

A few minutes later the custodian tried to free Tony's foot. He had no luck either.

Then Mrs. Hernandez, the principal, entered the rest room. Most kids called her The Terminator behind her back, but they called her Mrs. Hernandez to her face—so they wouldn't *get* terminated.

Tony's face turned red. He couldn't believe a woman was in the boys' rest room. He couldn't believe his foot was stuck in a toilet. But most of all, he couldn't believe his stupid human trick had flopped.

"Way to go, Tony," Mrs. Hernandez said. She leaned over and tugged on his leg. Tony's foot didn't budge. "Mo, tell my secretary to call 911."

"We're *really* dead now," muttered Mo as he headed to the office.

The rescue squad arrived within minutes. They quickly solved the problem. The water was turned off. The toilet was cut in half with a diamond-tipped saw. And Tony's foot was free once again.

Mr. Gore had to go home and change clothes.

Mrs. Hernandez's secretary had to watch Mr. Gore's class.

Tony and Mo had to go to the principal's office.

Mrs. Hernandez sat, tapping her fingers on her desk. "*Boys!* We are in Kansas City, not New York City. This is Riverview Elementary School, not the Ed Sullivan Theater. I'm in charge here, not David Letterman. I don't want any more nonsense. Do you understand?"

"Yes, ma'am."

"And you both may mop the boys' rest room after school—every day—for the rest of the week. Now get out of here. It's time for recess." Mrs. Hernandez grinned evilly. "And if I were you, I'd look out for Mr. Gore. He may *terminate* you when he gets back to school!"

News spread fast throughout Riverview Elementary School. Kids crowded around Tony and Mo at recess. They'd become heroes.

Anna Peterson walked up to the crowd of kids. Her hair was the color of gold. She always ate peanut butter and banana sandwiches for lunch. Everyone called her Anna Banana—for obvious reasons.

"Hi, guys," she said. "TB, you are one fabtastick guy. Will you still be my friend when you become famous?"

"Yeah, sure," he said, blushing for the second time that day. Anna was the prettiest girl in fifth grade.

"A few weeks ago I thought this deck would be the end of me," Mr. Madison sighed as he sat down in a wicker rocking chair, "but on a beautiful evening like this one, I can easily forget that building this baby was a major pain-in-the-donkey."

"Speaking of pains-in-the-donkey," said Maria, Tony's sixteen-year-old know-it-all sister, "I heard that a certain fifth grader"—she paused, shifted in her deck chair, and locked eyes with Tony—"was the King of Donkeys today."

"King of Donkeys!" exclaimed Tony. "No way. I'm the Future King of Late Night TV!"

"More like the *present* and *future* King of Stupid Huma—'"

"That's enough, Maria!" Mrs. Madison placed a tray of cookies and a pitcher of lemonade on the table. "Zip it, now, or you'll be the Queen of

Clean in about two minutes. If my memory serves me correctly, your palace is a disgrace to the kingdom."

"Good one, Mom," Tony said.

Maria glared at Tony.

"So, Tony," said Mr. Madison. "I understand that there was a bit of excitement at school today."

"Yeah, Dad. It was great! I'm on my way to national TV."

"Is that right?"

"Yeah, I'm going to start writing to David Letterman, send him some top ten lists, and tell him about my adventures. When he reads my letters, he'll invite me on his show."

"Well, Tony, Mrs. Hernandez didn't think that your adventure was so great."

"Mr. Gore, either," added Mrs. Madison.

"Yeah . . . well . . . I didn't mean for all of that to happen. I was just practicing my Stupid Human—"

Mr. Madison interrupted. "We know how much you love David Letterman, Tony. Maybe you will be on his show someday. But get there *carefully* . . . if you know what I mean."

"Yes," agreed Mrs. Madison. "We'll overlook

today's fiasco. No punishment . . . this time. But we make no promises for the future. Do you understand?"

"Yes, ma'am, I understand. No more rescue squads will be called to school because of me," said Tony. "But can you make one promise for me Mom?"

"What's that?"

"Will you please tape the *Late Show* for me?"

"You should tape *The Dork Show with Tony Dorkerman* instead," Maria mumbled.

"Maria!" Mrs. Madison warned. "Yes, Tony, I'll tape it for you."

"Thanks, Mom, you're the greatest."

"And me?" Mr. Madison smiled.

"You're the greatest, too, Dad."

Maria stood up. "If you will please excuse me. I have to go disgorge my stomach."

Maria made her usual grand exit.

"Hey, no problem. Have a good one." Tony reached for a cookie. "More cookies and lemonade for us!"

Later that night, Tony wrote a letter before he went to bed.

Dear Mr. Letterman,

I'm going to be on your show someday. I might even take over for you after you retire. Here's a top ten list you might want to use sometime.

THE TOP 10 WAYS TO RUIN THE FIRST DAY OF 5TH GRADE

10. Wear your pajamas to school instead of your favorite jeans and T-shirt.

9. Tell the rest of the class what a dork your teacher is when he is standing behind you.

8. Notice that your fly is down . . . after you've been in class for three hours.

7. Rush into the rest room, drop your pants, sit, and then realize you're in the wrong rest room.

6. Sneeze and accidentally blow boogers all over your teacher's desk.

5. Fall asleep in class and dream you're using the toilet.

4. Enjoy playing with building blocks on the first day of school, only to wonder why you are a giant compared to the rest of the kids in class.

3. Drop your lunch bag into an unflushed toilet.

2. Eat beans the night before the first day of school.
1. Get your foot stuck in a toilet in the boys' rest room and then have to be rescued by the 911 guys.

Sincerely,
Tony Baloney

P.S. #1 really happened to me. My phone number is 816-555-0942 (in case you want to invite me on your show). By the way, I also have a big space between my two front teeth. Don't tell my parents, but I will do anything to get on your show!

2.
Stupid Pet Tricks

Two weeks passed. Nothing happened. Mr. Gore didn't have to leave school to change his clothes. Mrs. Hernandez didn't have to call 911. And David Letterman didn't phone Tony. Everything was peaceful . . . until the first day of Pet Week.

Kids jabbered excitedly as they entered the classroom and took their seats.

The following message was printed neatly on the chalkboard:

DEAR KIDS: PLEASE REMEMBER THAT THIS IS PET WEEK. LET'S LEARN SOMETHING AND HAVE FUN WITH OUR ANIMALS. YOUR FRIEND, TOM

Dean Smith had a snake wrapped around his neck. Dean was the meanest kid in class. Everybody called him Mean Dean the Bully Machine—because he was a fifth-grade thug.

Anna had a tiny, black kitten climbing on her head.

Casey O'Neil had an empty birdcage on her desk. She was very forgetful. Everybody called her Spacey Casey—which wasn't totally true because she was the only kid in class who could do multiplication problems in her head.

And Tony had a fuzzy, white Pekingese with a flat face sitting on his lap. His dog looked as if it had run into a brick wall at sixty miles an hour.

"Quiet, class," Mr. Gore said, clapping his hands. "Welcome to Pet Week."

"Uh, Mr. G," someone yelled. "Meano Deano's face looks like a swollen blueberry. I think his head's going to pop!"

Mr. Gore walked over to Dean and took a closer look.

"Yes, I think you're right." He grabbed the snake and slowly unwound it from Dean's neck.

"It's about time, Mr. Gorilla," said Dean, gasping for air. "What took you so long?"

Mr. Gore said nothing, rolled his eyes, and then wrapped the snake back around Dean's neck.

The class cheered.

"As I was saying," continued Mr. Gore. "This week is special. Each of you will share your pet with the class. Today, Anna, Tony, and Casey will share their pets with us. And Dean might—if his head doesn't explode!"

Mr. Gore walked over to a large aquarium that was next to his desk. It was nearly as big as a bathtub. It had no fish in it, but was full of water.

"And I have a special surprise," he said, tapping the side of the aquarium. "Later today we'll get our own class pets. Anna's mom is bringing us ten goldfish."

The class cheered again.

"Let's get started. Tony, why don't you go first?"

Tony carried his white puffball to the front of the room.

"This is Meatball," said Tony. "He's going to make me famous."

"How?" asked Mike Elway, who had his finger

up his nose. Everybody called him Gold-digger—because he was a world-class nose picker.

"Stupid pet tricks," said Tony.

"What?" Mike continued to dig for gold.

"You know. Like on the *Late Show with David Letterman*. Sometimes people bring their pets on his show to do stupid pet tricks."

"So?" said Mike.

"So," said Tony, "someday Meatball and I will be on the show."

"Yeah, right." Mike wasn't convinced.

Mr. Gore was getting impatient. "Let's get started."

"My assistant will now get our props," said Tony.

Mo disappeared into the hallway and returned dragging a miniature trampoline. He placed it halfway between the door and Mr. Gore's desk. Then he pulled two bandannas out of his back pocket.

"TB, I don't like the looks of this." Mr. Gore's voice sounded funny.

"Don't worry," said Tony. "Everything's under control. My assistant will explain."

Mo bowed before the class. "Ladies and gentlemen: You will now see an amazing trick. I will blindfold Meatball. He will run and leap onto the trampoline, flip through the air, and then land in TB's arms. The real trick is that TB will also be blindfolded!"

"Wow!" said Anna as her kitten jumped onto Dean's head.

"Cool!" said Mike as he jammed his finger as far as possible up his nose.

"Beautiful," mumbled Casey as she stared at her empty birdcage.

"Stupid," gasped Dean as he struggled to free his head from the kitten and the snake.

"Exactly," said Tony. "*Stupid* Pet Tricks. David Letterman is really going to love this."

"I have the feeling that I won't." Mr. Gore folded his arms over his huge chest and then sat on a corner of his desk.

Mo blindfolded Tony and stood him next to Mr. Gore's desk, facing the trampoline.

Then Mo blindfolded Meatball and carried him out into the hallway. He placed the dog on the floor, facing the trampoline.

"Go!" said Mo.

Meatball raced into the classroom.

"Jump!" said Mo.

Meatball leaped into the air, came down, and landed perfectly on the trampoline.

He bounced off it and flipped through the air like an Olympic gymnast.

Tony waited with open arms.

Meatball missed Tony's open arms and sailed into the aquarium like a miniature cannonball. *Woosh!*

Unfortunately, Mr. Gore, his desk, and the floor all took a direct hit. Nothing was spared.

"Not again, Tony!" Mr. Gore yelled as he hopped off his desk. His feet shot out from under him and he landed with a thud on the wet floor.

Nobody made a sound. Not one kid. Not ten kids. Not any kids. The class just stared at Mr. G.

Then Anna broke the spell and ran up to the front of the room. "Fantabulous, TB," she said.

"Thanks." Tony couldn't see her, but he could smell her. She smelled sort of sweet, like baby shampoo. He loved the smell of baby shampoo. His heart beat like a drum and his face turned red.

"I'm going to get a job at McDonald's," Mr. Gore grunted, propping himself up on one elbow. "Flipping burgers has got to be safer."

An explosion of voices engulfed the classroom. "Will we get free fries?"

"How about milk shakes?"

"I want a million cheeseburgers."

"I want to meet Ronald McDonald!"

"I want to marry Ronald McDonald!"

Then The Terminator walked into the room.

All mouths immediately closed. All heads immediately turned toward Mrs. Hernandez. Even Meatball's.

I'm dead now, thought Tony as he pulled off his bandanna.

"What's going on in here?" Mrs. Hernandez asked. "Where's Mr. Gore?"

"I'm down here."

It only took Mrs. Hernandez ten seconds to figure out what was going on.

Mr. Gore had to go home and change clothes.

Mrs. Hernandez's secretary had to watch Mr. Gore's class.

Tony and Mo had to go to the principal's office.

That night at the dinner table Tony's mother asked, "Tony, why can't you watch cartoons like a normal kid?"

"I don't know, Mom." Tony slurped a spaghetti noodle into his mouth and tomato sauce splattered all over his chin.

"He's not normal. That's why," said Maria.

"Speaking of not normal!" said Tony. "It looks like somebody performed a nuclear test on your hair!" Maria had just made a fashionable change in hair color—from sun-bleached blonde to pukey reddish orange.

"That's enough. Both of you." Tony's father took a bite of garlic toast. Butter dripped onto his Kansas City Chiefs T-shirt. "As for you, Mr. Madison, Mrs. Hernandez informed me that you'll be missing recess for a week and will clean hamster cages instead. Was it worth it?"

"Well . . . I guess not." Tony hesitated.

"You *guess* not! Listen closely, young man. I don't want any more calls from Mrs. Hernandez. Do you understand?"

"Yes, sir," said Tony.

"And, Maria. Please boycott future nuclear tests on your hair."

"Yes, sir," said Maria.

"May I be excused?" asked Tony. "I'm going to go write another letter to David Letterman."

"Yes, you may," said Tony's mother. "After you load the dishwasher. And for your information, you'll be doing the dishes by yourself—all week. And I suggest that you don't test our patience any further."

"Yes, ma'am."

"Keep up the good work, TB," Maria snickered. "Maybe I'll never have to do the dishes again!"

Tony stuck his tongue out at Maria. "Mom, would you mail my letter first thing tomorrow?"

"You write it; I'll mail it."

"Thanks."

September 20

Dear Mr. Letterman,

Did you get my first letter? I hope so. My dog, Meatball, and I are dying to be on your show. We're ready for Stupid Pet Tricks. Here's another top ten list you might want to use sometime.

THE TOP 10 SIGNS YOUR 5TH GRADE TEACHER IS HAVING A BAD DAY

10. During break time, he drinks out of a coffee mug and forgets that it's full of tempera paint and then says: "Mmm . . . best coffee I ever had!"
9. During PE, he sends the class to Toys "Я" Us.
8. During math, he insists that $8 + 9 = 89$.
7. During social studies, he insists that Disney World is the capital of the United States.
6. During science, he insists that babies come from Mars.

5. During reading, he insists that Harry Potter is really "You Know Who."
4. During a faculty meeting, he calls the principal "The Terminator" instead of her real name.
3. During an art lesson, he staples his tongue to the bulletin board instead of your class's projects.
2. During homeroom, he fills out the school attendance slip and writes his name on the top of the "absent list."
1. During "Pet Week" he takes a shower in class instead of at home.

Sincerely,
Tony Baloney

P.S. #1 really happened. Call me and I'll explain. My phone number is 816-555-0942. I can't wait to be on your show! By the way, my mom tapes your show for me and I watch it after school every day. And when I'm really bored, I watch old *Late Show* afternoon reruns on cable.

3.
World War III

"Mo." Tony took a bite of his peanut butter and baloney sandwich. "I don't think David Letterman is ever going to call."

"Sure he will," said Mo.

"But it's been four weeks since I mailed him my first letter."

"He probably gets a million letters a day. It'll take him a while to read yours. He'll call."

Tony stuck his finger into his mouth and scraped bread, baloney, and peanut butter from the roof. "I don't know. Maybe I really need to get his attention."

Mo picked up a mushy french fry and wriggled it. He ignored Tony's remark. "I hate cafeteria food. Maybe I'll start bringing my lunch."

Tony took his finger out of his mouth and studied the glob of goo stuck on the end. "Did you hear me?"

Mo looked deep into Tony's eyes. "Yes, I did. And that worries me."

Tony licked the goo off his finger. He stood up and took a quick look around the cafeteria. Ms. Grant, the lunch monitor, was nowhere in sight. Maybe she went to the rest room. Maybe she took a kid to the nurse. Maybe she went to The Terminator's office. Maybe she went to the moon. It didn't matter. She was gone.

Tony shouted, "Mo, watch this." He lifted the bun off Mo's hamburger. He picked up the patty. Mean Dean sat on the other side of the cafeteria.

"Oh, no." Mo covered his eyes.

"Oh, yes." Tony cocked his wrist, narrowed his eyes, and sent the hamburger patty flying through the air like a Frisbee.

The patty smacked the back of Dean's head and exploded upon impact. Ketchup and mustard flew everywhere.

Dean stood up and slowly turned around. Ketchup and mustard oozed down the back of his neck.

Tony waved at him.

"This means war, Baloney!" Dean yelled.

Dean picked up a patty and fired it at Tony.

Tony ducked. It hit Daisy Buck in the face. This was unfortunate because Daisy was the sort of student who once ate thirteen crayons just to see if it could be done. Everybody called her Crazy Daisy—even her mother.

Daisy wiped ketchup and mustard out of her eyes. She scanned the cafeteria until she saw Dean. "Enemy sighted. Prepare to launch missiles!"

"Hit the deck!" Mo yelled. "Crazy Daisy's on the loose."

"Fire missile number one!" She heaved her milk cartoon at Dean. Milk showered the cafeteria as it flew through the air.

Then she picked up the milk carton to her left. "Fire missile number two!" Kids scrambled for cover. Silence fell over the cafeteria.

"Fire missile number three!" she yelled as she picked up the milk carton to her right and fired it at the enemy. It hit the wall and exploded above Dean's head.

Then General Casey climbed on the table and yelled, "Fire all missiles!"

"Bombs away!" someone yelled. That's all it took. Within seconds milk cartons, hamburger patties, and mushy french fries were flying in all directions. The cafeteria rumbled with the sounds of combat. It was a battle zone—World War III.

Tony looked at the remaining piece of food on Mo's tray. JELL-O—a rectangular blob of jiggling cherry JELL-O. The perfect weapon to end the perfect battle, he thought.

He quickly gathered his friends around him. "This is it," he said, picking up a piece of JELL-O. "Grab a chunk and let's bomb the Bully Machine."

Something touched him on the shoulder. Something nice. Something soft. That something was Anna Banana's hand.

"Count me in, TB," said Anna as she took her hand off his shoulder and then slugged him.

Tony rubbed his arm. His face turned as red as the JELL-O, "Thanks," was all he could manage as a goofy grin spread across his face.

Mo elbowed Tony. "Snap out of it, Romeo. It's time to blast the Bully Machine."

"Uh . . . yeah . . . uh . . . right. Where is he?" Tony asked.

"Over by the hallway door," said Mo.

"Let's go," said Tony.

Tony and his team crouched low and closed in on their target. Dean was leaning against the cafeteria door. When they got within striking distance, they stopped.

"On the count of three," whispered Tony. "One, two, three. Fire!"

Tony's soldiers jumped up and fired their JELL-O. Red jiggling missiles rocketed through the air. It was a beautiful sight.

Dean ducked just before impact. As the missiles flew over Dean's head, the door opened, and Mr. Gore stepped into the cafeteria. *Splat!* Slimy blobs of JELL-O slammed into Mr. Gore. His face. His huge chest. His belly. His legs. Nothing was spared.

Mo looked at Tony. Tony looked at Mo. "We're dead," they said at the same time.

Mr. Gore was stunned. He was also a mess. But most of all he was mad. End-of-the-world mad. "Anthony Madison and Mohammad bin Abdul Hamad bin Jamaluddin bin al-Rashid! I'm going to ship you both back to kindergarten!"

Mr. Gore had to go home and change clothes.

Mrs. Hernandez's secretary had to watch the kids clean up the cafeteria.

Tony and Mo had to go to the principal's office.

Mrs. Hernandez tapped her pen on her desk and glared at the two boys sitting across from her. The silence seemed to last forever. Both boys squirmed in their chairs. Then she finally spoke. "Why?"

"Well," Tony timidly began. "I saw this great food fight—"

"On the *Late Show with David Letterman,*" Mrs. Hernandez interrupted. "Right?"

"Yeah, it was really—"

"Unnecessary," Mrs. Hernandez interrupted again.

She continued to glare at them. Her eyes looked like a cobra's. Slitted. Dangerous. "Boys, I've had enough of this *Late Show* nonsense. You're both on cafeteria cleanup duty for a month. I don't want to see you in here again. Do you understand?"

"Yes, ma'am," both boys answered.

"If I see you in here again, I may have to suspend you from school for a day. Now scram," Mrs. Hernandez hissed through her gritted teeth. "And if I were you, I'd beg for mercy when Mr. Gore gets back. He just may *terminate* you."

Mr. Gore didn't terminate the two boys. So later that night, after promising his parents that he wouldn't be the one to start World War IV, Tony wrote a letter to David Letterman before he went to bed.

Dear Mr. Letterman,

Did you get my letters yet? I hope so. Do you like peanut butter and baloney sandwiches? I love them. Here's another top ten list you might want to use on your show.

THE TOP 10 WAYS TO SURPRISE YOUR 5TH GRADE TEACHER

10. Actually turn your homework in when it's due.
9. Wear prison uniforms to class.
8. Set him up on a blind date with Miss America.
7. Post a photo of him—collecting the morning newspaper in his underwear—on the school website.
6. Call him Dad and insist that you're really his kid.
5. Fill his cup of coffee with tabasco sauce.
4. Hang his underwear on the class Christmas tree instead of ornaments.
3. Tell him you love school more than Toys "Я" Us.
2. Paper clip a ten dollar bill to a note saying, "Thanks," and give it to him before you turn in a test you forgot to study for.

1. Bomb him with JELL-O chunks when he walks into the cafeteria.

Sincerely,
Tony Baloney

P.S. #1 really happened. I got in big trouble today and now I'm on cafeteria cleanup duty at school. My dad was really mad at me. He threatened to have some MPs from Leavenworth come and cart me away because I was involved in a sort-of-like military operation at school today. And my mom wasn't too happy, either. She was so mad at me that she wouldn't talk to me, so she wrote me a note and taped it to my bedroom door. It said:

Mr. Anthony Madison,
Congratulations! Because of events that occurred today, your allowance will not be automatically deposited into your grimy fist for the next week.

Best Regards,
Your mother

Call me and I'll explain. My phone number is 816-555-0942. Please invite me to be on your show. Soon! Before I end up in a military prison!

4.
The Photocopy

"No way," Mo insisted.

"Come on," Tony pleaded.

"No way. Mr. G will kill me. The Terminator will kill me. My parents will kill me."

"Nobody will kill you because nobody's going to find out." Tony emptied the teachers' work-room paper-recycling bin into a large plastic bag. "We're *supposed* to be in here. Remember? Mr. G's orders."

"He told us to empty *all* of the school's bins *and* not to goof off while we're at it," Mo replied. "And then meet our class in art. Let's get out of here. This place gives me the creeps."

"This will only take a couple of minutes," Tony pleaded. "*And* there aren't any teachers in here. We won't have another chance like this in a million years."

"You're crazy, TB. It's only been a week since the food fight. Won't you ever give up?"

"Never," Tony said. "I'm on a mission. And when my mission succeeds, we'll both be famous."

"Yeah. We'll be famous dead guys," Mo mumbled. "Let's get this over with before a teacher shows up."

Tony opened the door and looked both ways. There were no snotty-nosed kindergartners bopping down the hallway. There were no janitors mopping the shiny floor. There were no stupid fourth graders picking on whiny first graders. And best of all, there was no Terminator to be seen.

"The coast is clear. It's time to rock and roll," Tony said.

"Rock and roll? I think it's time for heads to roll—*ours,*" said Mo, drawing his forefinger across his neck. "I should have my head examined . . . while I still have it."

"Don't forget," said Tony as he lifted the lid to the photocopy machine. "You're going to be famous."

"Yeah. Right. Just hurry up!"

Tony dropped his pants to his ankles. He looked around the room, took a deep breath, and dropped his Fruit Of The Looms to his ankles. Then he hopped up on the photocopy machine and planted his bare bottom on the glass.

"Press the green button, Mo."

"How about if I press the I'm-as-good-as-dead button?" Mo pushed the green button. The machine whirred into action. Mo picked up the copy, looked at it, and then handed it to Tony. "Looks like the back end of a jacka—"

"Fantastic! A perfect shot of my hinder," Tony proudly interrupted. "Now press the two button, the five button, and then the green button."

"Twenty-five copies!" Mo said, a look of dread on his face. "That will take forever."

"I'll give them out as souvenirs when I become famous."

"I should have known," said Mo. The machine whirred into action again.

Mo looked at the door. He fiddled with the collar of his shirt. He wiped the sweat trickling down his forehead.

Tony smiled at Mo and asked, "Are you having fun yet?"

Mo ignored him.

Everything was okay at five copies. No problem at ten copies. The machine shot out fifteen copies and success seemed to be just around the corner. But at nineteen copies the door began to open slowly.

Mo whispered, "TB, the door. We're dead now."

Tony held his breath, while Mo stood as still as a statue. The door opened a couple of inches. Then another inch. Fingers curled around the edge of the door. Long fingers. Adult fingers. Tony stared at the diamond ring on one of the fingers. He'd seen that ring before—on The Terminator's hand! Fear raced through his body. The end was near.

The door opened a full six inches. Then the hand disappeared and the door swung shut.

Tony let his breath out with a rush. Mo slid to the floor and sat on his backside. And the machine spit out the last copy.

"Whew. That was close," Tony said, hopping down from the copier.

"Too close," said Mo, scrambling to his feet. "Let's get out of here."

Tony pulled up his Fruit Of The Looms, his

pants, and then grabbed the stack of photocopies. He opened the door and stuck his head into the hallway. "Nobody in sight. Follow me."

He slipped out of the teachers' workroom with Mo following close behind. "I can't believe we made it," Mo whispered.

"We'd better empty the rest of the bins," said Tony. "Before Mr. G comes looking for us."

The two boys zipped down the hallway in search of the next recycling bin. They rounded the first corner of the hallway and crashed into Mr. Gore (who was leading a class to art). *Whamo!* Photocopies of Tony's hinder flew into the air and fluttered to the floor. Red paint shot out of a bucket Mr. Gore was carrying. The paint geyser splattered Mr. Gore from head to foot. His class, lined up like perfect little angels, stood in stunned silence.

Mr. Gore calmly placed the paint bucket on the floor. He didn't scream at the boys. He didn't say a single word. He just arched his eyebrows, curled his lips into an evil grin, and drew his forefinger across his neck.

Then his class went totally nuts as they scrambled to pick up the copies.

"Look—a photocopy of Mean Dean's face!"

"Naw. It's a copy of Daisy's twin brother!"

"No way. It's Mrs. Hernandez!"

"You're all wrong. It's a copy of Mr. G's cheeks. Sort of puffy. Like a chipmunk's!"

"Naw. It's a copy of someone's *other* set of cheeks!"

Mo put his hands in his pockets and leaned against the wall. "We're goners, TB."

"Yes, the end is near," Tony said, joining Mo. "We almost made it. Anyway, it's been great—"

"Don't worry, TB." Anna joined the two boys by the wall. "I'll never let anything happen to you."

Then she leaned close to Tony. Her breath smelled fresh. Minty fresh. Like a new piece of peppermint gum. Tony loved peppermint gum. A swarm of butterflies seemed to take flight in his stomach. He looked down at the floor and stammered: "Uh, gee . . . thanks, Anna."

She shoved a photocopy in his face and said, "Great show, TB! Will you please autograph your glutimous maximillius for me?"

"Yeah, sure," Tony muttered, his face turning red. "How did you know it was mine?"

Anna winked at Tony and said, "I'll never tell."

Mr. Gore had to go home and change clothes.

Mrs. Hernandez's secretary had to take the kids to art.

Tony and Mo had to go to the principal's office.

Later that night Tony sat through a very uncomfortable dinner. Nobody said a word. His parents didn't even look at him. Maria occasionally sneered, but that was normal. At least the silent treatment was better than getting killed, he thought.

After dinner his mom and dad did the dishes. That was really weird because Tony and Maria always did the supper dishes. Tony's stomach spun like a top. Maybe his parents *were* going to kill him.

After the dishes were finished, the Madisons settled into their favorite positions in the living room to watch the news: Mr. Madison in his recliner, Mrs. Madison in her rocker, Maria on the couch, and Tony on the floor.

Nobody had turned on the TV, so Tony got up to find the remote.

"Sit down," Tony's father said. "The news will have to wait for a bit tonight."

The Madisons always watched the news every night after dinner. It was a family tradition.

Tony's time had come. He slowly sank to the floor.

His father got up and circled the living room like a vulture. He stopped and stared down at Tony. "Why? May I ask why?"

"Well . . . be—"

"Because he's just a fifth grader," interrupted Maria in her you're-just-a-dork-and-I'm-way-cooler sixteen-year-old way. "He's so embarrassing."

"As if you're not," Tony snorted. "You're beginning to look like a human Christmas tree with all those things hanging on you." Maria had just made a major fashion statement: a pierced right nostril and a pierced left eyebrow—both sporting shiny gold hoops—to go along with her multi-pierced ears.

Maria picked up an overstuffed couch pillow and fired it at Tony. It hit him in the back of the head.

Tony pulled off his sock, tied a quick knot in it, and fired it at Maria. It smacked her between the eyes. "Bull's-eye!"

"That's enough. Both of you," Mr. Madison ordered. Then he locked eyes with Tony. "Well? Why did Mrs. Hernandez have to call us *again*?

Why do you have to spend your recesses writing a report about the history of photocopy machines? And why will you be suspended from school if you get sent to her office one more time? Well?"

"There was this lady on the *Late Show* the other day. She photocopied her face. David Letterman really made a big deal out of it. He fired copies of her face into the audience. It was pretty funny. So, I figured I'd do the same thing. And then give the copies to my fans when I become—"

"This is ridiculous," Mrs. Madison interrupted as she got up from her rocker and joined Mr. Madison. Both towered above Tony. "I'm sick of this nonsense. Drop it. Now. I'm not taping the show for you anymore. And there will be no more letters to David Letterman. Or you may never see the light of day again . . . because I'll get to you before Mr. Gore or Mrs. Hernandez does. Have I made myself clear?"

"Yes, ma'am," Tony muttered.

Mr. Madison said, "I want all of your old *Late Show* tapes, and I want two *perfect* letters of apology written tonight before you go to bed. One for Mr. Gore and the other for Mrs. Hernandez.

You'll give the letters to each—personally—before school tomorrow morning. *And* I want to see the letters before you go to sleep. Starting tomorrow, you can forget about playing after school. You'll be spending your time in the yard—raking and bagging leaves—*by yourself,* for however many days it takes to finish the job. *And* if this happens again, I'll get to you before Mr. Gore, Mrs. Hernandez, or your mother does. Do you understand?"

"Yes, sir."

"As for you, Maria. No more holes in your body. You're starting to look like a human pincushion."

"Yes, sir."

"Now turn on the news. I want to catch the stock report."

After the news, Tony wrote his apologies and gathered his old *Late Show* tapes. He gave his tapes to his dad and showed him the letters. His dad said they were A-OK and then sent Tony to bed. Tony lay in bed and stared at the ceiling. Only one thing was on his mind: the *Late Show*. He climbed out of bed and went to his desk and began writing his third letter of the night.

Dear Mr. Letterman,

I saw the photocopy stunt on your show the other night. It was so cool I decided to try my own photocopy stunt at school. It backfired and I got into big trouble. Oh, well. Here's another top ten list you might want to use sometime.

THE TOP 10 THINGS YOU SHOULD NEVER DO AT SCHOOL

10. Eat the three-month-old peanut butter and jelly sandwich that you found in the back of your desk.

9. Drop the frog (that you dissected in science class) into your teacher's cup of coffee.

8. Stick your tongue in the automatic pencil sharpener.

7. Barf on your teacher's desk instead of in the garbage can.

6. Ask your PE teacher if he's ever heard of deodorant.

5. Use the classroom's pet hamster as a chalkboard eraser.

4. Write test answers on your forehead with a permanent marker.

3. Ask your principal if she graduated from the Ringling Bros. and Barnum & Bailey Clown College.
2. See how far you can stick a crayon up your nose.
1. Copy your hinder on the school's photocopy machine.

Sincerely,
Tony Baloney

P.S. #1 really happened. Yes, I copied my own hinder and it was a disaster. Call me and I'll explain. My phone number is 816-555-0942. My dad confiscated all of my old *Late Show* tapes, and my mom won't tape any more shows for me. I've secretly mailed this letter to you. My parents don't know about it. If they find out, I'm a goner. Please invite me to be on your show before it is too late.

5.

Can a Boy in a Bear Suit Disrupt a Professional Football Game?

"Mom, I want to be a bear for Halloween," said Tony.

"A bear?"

"Yeah. A bear."

"Why can't you be a ghost? Or a vampire?" Mrs. Madison placed a plate of steaming pancakes on the kitchen table.

Tony forked a couple of pancakes, dropped them onto his plate, and drowned them with maple syrup. "Because bears are undeniably the coolest creatures on planet Earth."

"Says who?"

"Me," Tony said, lifting a bite of pancake toward his mouth. A thin string of syrup stretched between his fork and plate. Tony broke the string with his tongue.

"Well . . . Mr. Me," said Mrs. Madison, "bears may be cool, but there's more to this than you're telling me. Something's been bugging you for the last few days. Moms know these things. What's up, Mr. Me?"

Tony shrugged his shoulders.

"Come on, TB. My mom radar is pretty strong. It tells me that there are two things bothering you. Number one: I think you're upset because your father and I came down hard on you after you photocopied your back end. Number two: I don't think you want to be a bear for Halloween because they're cool. This has something to do with that TV show, doesn't it?"

Tony stared into his plate. Should he come totally clean and lay it all out before his mother? Or should he *sort of* lay it all out before his mother? He opted for sort of.

"Well . . . Mom," Tony slowly said, "raking leaves isn't so bad, but missing the *Late Show* is torture. You sure know how to hurt a guy."

"Well, Mr. Me, I didn't photocopy my butt.

You did. So now you have to deal with the consequences. I didn't hurt you; you hurt yourself."

"I guess you're right."

"Now . . . what about the bear suit? Is there a *Late Show* connection?"

"Not really," Tony said, choosing his words carefully. "I saw a guy wear a bear suit on the *Late Show* once, but it was no big deal."

"No big deal, huh? And if I rent a bear suit for you, will it turn into a big deal?"

"How could it, Mom? Come on. It's just Halloween. It seems to me that you're the one making a big deal out of this. All I want is for my costume to be different from everyone else's. Is there anything wrong with that? And . . . don't forget, bears are undeniably the coolest creatures on planet Earth!"

"No, there's nothing wrong with wanting to be different," Mrs. Madison chuckled, "and bears *are* cool!"

"No, you're cool, Mom," Tony said as he shoved a bite of pancake into his mouth, "even though you're tougher than a prison warden."

Mrs. Madison looked at Tony and smiled. "So, Mr. Me, where am I going to get a bear costume? They aren't common, you know."

"Remember that costume shop down at the Plaza? I bet you could rent one there. I'd even chip in some of my allowance money."

"Your own money. Hmmm," Mrs. Madison said, sipping her coffee. "You are serious about this, aren't you?"

"Yes, ma'am."

"Okay. I'll rent one. But promise that you'll take good care of it."

Tony got up and went over to his mother, grabbed her fingers, drew them to his lips, and kissed the back of her hand. "I promise, Madame, that I will do nothing to disgrace your royal name," he muttered in his best British accent.

"Oh, brother," Mrs. Madison sighed, wiping the sticky mess off her hand. "Why don't I believe you?"

"Smells good," Mr. Madison interrupted as he wandered into the kitchen. "Where's Maria?"

"She'll be in bed till noon. You know how Saturdays and teenagers are," Mrs. Madison answered.

Mr. Madison snatched a piece of bacon from the plateful on the counter. "So what's new with you, TB?" he asked.

"Two things," answered Tony as he sat back down to his pancakes. "I'm going to be a bear for Halloween and I'm going to a Chiefs football game."

Mr. Madison raised his eyebrows. "Did you say a Chiefs game?" The Kansas City Chiefs were his favorite football team.

"Yeah. My class is going on a special field trip. I forgot to tell you about it. We get to see the Chiefs play the New York Jets next weekend—on Halloween Day. Any kid who wears a costume gets a team picture of the Chiefs. Mr. Gore got free tickets from the quarterback. They played together in college. Anyway, Mr. Gore says we might even get to meet some of the players and get their autographs. It's going to be great!"

"Free tickets? Autographs? Wow!" said Mr. Madison.

"Please, please, please don't forget to sign my permission form."

"I won't," Mr. Madison assured Tony.

"Do you think you can go, too? Mr. Gore needs some parent volunteers."

"You know I'd love to . . ." Mr. Madison mumbled, with a dreamy look on this face, "more than anything. But your mother and I volunteered to sponsor the Halloween party at the children's hospital. You go ahead and have a great time."

"I will, Dad."

"You are one lucky guy," sighed Mr. Madison. "That should be a heck of a game."

A slight chill hung in the air. Puffy clouds drifted across the deep blue sky. Red, orange, and gold leaves fluttered to and fro on their journey to the ground.

A yellow school bus, packed with noisy kids and a handful of parent volunteers, pulled into the parking lot of Arrowhead Stadium. Mr. Gore herded his class off the bus and gathered them around himself. "We're in for a real treat today," he said. "The Chiefs and the Jets are both undefeated. This should be a classic NFL battle."

"I hope the Jets crush the Chiefs," Dean muttered. "The Chiefs stink. They're just a bunch of wimps."

Mr. Gore gave Dean the evil eye.

"Class, please do three things today. Respect people. Respect property. And enjoy the game," Mr. Gore said. "This is going to be a blast."

"Look, Mr. Gore. I brought my baseball glove."

Spacey Casey beamed. "Maybe I'll catch a foul ball today."

Mr. Gore ruffled Casey's hair. "You might just do that, Batwoman," he laughed. "Let's go."

Mr. Gore and Casey led the way into Arrowhead Stadium. Tony slowly scanned the stadium. He couldn't believe how big it was. It reminded him of a giant bowl filled with people instead of cereal.

"Wow! How many people does this place hold?" he asked, adjusting his bear head from his right hand to his left hand.

"Duh," Dean replied. "About a million."

"Dean . . . cool it," Mr. Gore warned as he led them to their seats. "TB, it holds just over seventy-nine thousand people. And today is a sellout crowd. This place will be crazy in a short while."

Mr. G's class settled into section 119—right behind the Chiefs bench. Moms, dads, monsters, aliens, ninjas, ghosts, pirates, hobos, witches, and assorted others—normal and strange—quickly filled the stadium.

The Jets took the opening kickoff and promptly marched down the field, scored a touchdown, and made the extra point. Jets 7, Chiefs 0.

The Chiefs answered the challenge and grounded out seventy-seven yards to the Jets ten-yard line. On the next play they scored a touchdown on a beautiful quarterback sneak by Brent Green. Mr. Gore jumped up out of his seat and threw his popcorn into the air. "Did you see that?" he shouted. "What a drive! What a qb sneak by Green! I played college ball with that guy!" The Chiefs kicked the point after the touchdown. Jets 7, Chiefs 7.

Crazy Daisy, dressed as a soldier, spied the fluffy white popcorn kernels showering the people below Mr. Gore. It didn't take her long to move into action. She hopped up on her seat and yelled, "Fire away." Then she launched her box of popcorn as far as she could.

Mike Elway pulled his finger out of his clown nose, saluted Daisy, and threw *his* box of popcorn toward the heavens. "Cool," he mumbled.

Mo, Anna, and Tony stood in their seats. "On the count of three," cried Anna. "One, two, three!" And three more boxes of popcorn flew out over the crowd.

Within seconds, Arrowhead Stadium went nuts. Thousands of boxes of popcorn were launched toward the playing field. A blizzard of popcorn settled over the stadium. "Orville Redenbacher would have been proud," Mo said in awe as he viewed the snowless snowstorm.

Mr. Gore glared at Daisy, Mike, Mo, Anna, and Tony. "I hope you are proud of yourselves. Look at this mess."

They shrugged their shoulders.

"Uh . . . you started it," Tony said hesitantly.

Mr. Gore shook his head, rolled his eyes, and turned his attention back to the field.

The game rolled on. Both teams surged up and down the field. It was a Wild West sort of game.

At halftime the score was tied. Chiefs 21, Jets 21. At the end of three quarters the score was still tied. Chiefs 31, Jets 31.

But things weren't going well for the Chiefs in the fourth quarter. They couldn't score. Late in the quarter, the Jets were ahead. Jets 37, Chiefs 31. And the Jets were driving deep into Chiefs territory for yet another score. It didn't look good for the home team. Fortunately, the Jets fumbled the ball and the Chiefs recovered it on their own ten-yard line. Then the referee called the two-minute warning time-out.

"Ha, they'll never go ninety yards for a touchdown—in less than two minutes," Dean announced. "The game is over. I told you they were a bunch of wimps."

Everyone ignored Dean.

Tony nudged Mo. "It's time. Are you going with me?"

"Where?"

"I'm going to snatch the football from the field. Then I'll get it autographed by the Chiefs after the game."

"Yeah. Right."

"I'm really going," insisted Tony.

"Without me," said Mo, shoving a bite of cotton candy into his mouth. "I like living."

"Fine. I'll go by myself," said Tony.

"You're nuts."

"I might be. But who cares. I'll see you after the game."

Mo gave the thumbs-up sign to Tony and said, "Good luck. Because you'll need it."

"Thanks," Tony said as he stood up. Then he yelled down the row to Mr. Gore. "May I go to the urination station?"

"Yeah, sure," Mr. Gore answered.

"I'll take him," volunteered Mrs. Peterson,

sitting a few seats down from Mr. Gore. "Anna, do you need to go?"

"No, Ma."

"Okay, let's go, TB."

"Thanks," said Mr. Gore. He turned his attention to the ice-cream cone that Daisy had just dropped in his lap. And Tony and Mrs. Peterson worked their way up the steps toward the rest rooms.

"I'm going to step into the women's room," said Mrs. Peterson. "I'll meet you out front in three minutes."

"Thanks, Mrs. P," said Tony. "I'll be out in a flash."

Mrs. Peterson disappeared into the women's room, and Tony slipped back down the stairs toward the field.

A loud roar erupted from the fans when he reached the railing that separated the stands from the playing field. All eyes were on the field.

He hooked his leg over the rail and was ready to drop onto the field when somebody tapped him on the shoulder. Tony turned slowly around, expecting to see a very upset Mr. G. But this was not the case.

"I'm going," said a ninja.

"Me, too," said a princess.

"Mo and Anna! Wow! Let's go. Quick!"

"There's a problem, though, TB," said Anna, pointing to a nearby security guard on the back side of the sideline, just below the kids. "How are you going to get past him?"

Tony swung his leg back over the rail. "Good question. Any ideas?"

"I have an idea," said Mo. "Watch this."

"This better be good," said Tony. "If you mess up, my plan will be dead. Any maybe you, too."

"I have this one covered," Mo said, smiling at Tony. "Even *I* can come up with a good one from time to time."

"Yeah, right," said Tony.

"Have faith in your ol' buddy Mo, TB. Watch this." Mo curled his tongue, stuck his forefinger and thumb against his teeth, and let loose with a shrill whistle. The security guard turned and looked at him. "Excuse me, sir," yelled Mo, motioning to the security guard. "Can you please come over here?"

The guard made his way to Mo and looked up at him. "What's up, kid?"

"I don't know if I should report this or not, sir," Mo said, "but some guy in the first row, about three sections down, keeps throwing stuff down on the sideline. Someone might get hurt. I just thought you might want to know."

"You're darn right I want to know. I'll go check it out right away. Thanks, kid."

The guard hustled away and Mo smiled at Tony. "I told you I had it covered."

Tony clapped Mo on the back. "Darn good job, ol' buddy."

"What are we waiting for?" asked Anna. "The coast is clear."

"Yeah," said Tony. "Let's do it."

The three kids dropped down to the back of the sideline. Nobody noticed them because the security guard was looking for the out-of-control guy and the Chiefs had just moved to the fifty-yard line on a forty-yard pass. The people in the stands cheered wildly. The Chiefs coaches and players cheered wildly. The whole state of Missouri was probably cheering wildly.

The Jets called a time-out.

And the football sat all alone in the middle of the field.

Tony stared at the ball.

He put on his bear head. "Stay here and wait for me."

Then the short bundle of brown fur slipped through a gap of excited players and ran onto the football field.

Tony reached the middle of the field and grabbed the football. He turned and ran back toward the gap that would lead to safety. As he neared the sideline, the line judge stepped into his path and yelled, "What are you doing, bear?"

Tony cut to his right and streaked down the sideline. The zebra-striped line judge followed in hot pursuit.

"Give me that ball! Now!" yelled the line judge.

"No way," Tony cried.

Tony ran for his life.

The line judge ran after Tony.

And a voice boomed over the stadium loud-speaker. "The bear's at the forty-five. The forty. Look at him go!"

People in the stadium started chanting. "Go! Go! Go!"

Tony veered toward the center of the field. He chanced a quick look over his shoulder. He still had the lead. But when he looked back down the field he saw that trouble was waiting for him at the thirty-yard line—a large security guard in a dark blue uniform.

There was only one thing Tony could do. He ran straight at the guard. The guard waited with outstretched arms. At the last moment Tony cut left and then sharp to the right. The guard dove for Tony—but a second too late. All he got was an armful of grass as he lay face down on the thirty-yard line.

And the loudspeaker boomed again. "What a move by the bear! He's at the twenty-five. The twenty. Look at him go."

The crowd went bonkers. The stadium rocked with their chant. "GO, BEAR, GO! GO, BEAR, GO!"

Tony ran for all he was worth.

"He's at the fifteen! He's at the ten! Oh, no. The zebra's gaining on the bear," the loudspeaker boomed.

At the five-yard line the line judge dove for Tony, nicked the back of his right heel, and sent him flying. Tony flipped through the air and landed on his feet in the end zone.

"The bear scored a TD! The bear just scored a fifty-yard TD!" the loudspeaker boomed again.

Tony ran to the back of the end zone, took off his bear head, and performed a touchdown dance. The fans in the stands chanted, yelled, laughed, and threw their boxes of popcorn one more time. The second blizzard of the day hit Arrowhead Stadium.

Mo and Anna ran into the end zone and gave Tony a high five.

A camera crew followed them. A guy shoved a microphone into Tony's face. "Hey, kid. I'm from ESPN. Can I talk to you?"

"Yeah, sure," Tony panted, wiping sweat from his forehead.

"What's your name?"

"Anthony Madison. But my friends call me Tony Baloney or TB—for short."

"What a run, TB! What was that all about?"

"Well . . . it's about the *Late Show with David Letterman*," Tony answered.

"I don't understand," said the news guy.

"I saw this gag on the *Late Show* one night. A guy in a bear suit went out onto Broadway and tried to hail cabs, and then he tried to get hugs from strangers. It was really funny. So I thought I would wear a bear suit and try to snatch a football from an NFL game."

"Well, you did it, TB. What's next?"

"I'm going to be on the *Late Show* someday," Tony said. Then he put his arms around Anna's and Mo's shoulders. "And I'm going to take my two best friends with me."

"Thanks, TB," said Mo. "I'll go with you if I'm still alive after tonight."

"Thanks, TB," said Anna. "You *really* are the best." Then she put her arm around his waist and gave him a little squeeze. Tony's face turned bright red. As red as a Kansas City Chiefs uniform.

The news guy continued. "This is quite a story, but—"

"But this interview is over," interrupted Mr. Gore. "Out of the end zone kids. It's time to let the Chiefs do their thing."

He led Tony, Mo, and Anna to the Chiefs bench. The rest of the class and the parent volunteers were waiting for them—surrounded by giant football players. "I've received permission for us to watch the rest of the game from the sideline. It's delayed for fifteen minutes until all of the confusion is sorted out. Anna and Mo, take a seat. And Mr. Confusion, step over here with me."

Mr. Gore led Tony to the end of the bench and jerked Tony's bear head out of his hand and dangled it in front of him. "TB, I should have *your* head in my hand, not this stupid bear head. I think I'm going to send you to the locker room with one of the security guards until the game is over, and then I'll deal with you—"

"Tom, what are you doing down here?" a player asked as he passed by Mr. Gore and Tony.

Mr. Gore diverted his attention from Tony to the player. "Hey, Brent," Mr. Gore said as they shook hands, "that was an awesome sneak! And, unfortunately"—Mr. Gore paused and looked down at Tony—"what I'm doing *down here* is dealing with my own ten-year-old sneak."

Brent Green looked at Tony and smiled. "That was a heck of a run, kid! Maybe someday you'll play for the Chiefs. Your teacher was a heck of a player in college. He could have made the pros if it wasn't for that nasty knee injury he got his senior year. It's good to see you on the field again, Tom. Brings back good memories."

"That it does," said Mr. Gore.

"Hey, man. I have to get to my coach ASAP," Brent said as a wide smile creased his face, "or else I might soon find myself playing for the Bengals, and what a nightmare that would be. I don't want to mess with Coach Mitchell; he's a tough guy."

"That he is, Brent. You better get to the sideline," said Mr. Gore. "And do me a favor, would you? Pull off your two-minute magic and teach the Jets a lesson."

"Will do," Brent said. "I have my lucky game socks on. I haven't washed them since we made the play-offs last year."

"Disgusting," said Tony.

Brent tapped Tony's shoulder with his helmet. Then Brent Green and Mr. Gore made a fist with their right hands and brought them together in a light punch. "See you after the game," Brent said as he walked away.

Mr. Gore ruffled Tony's sweaty hair and winked at him. "Let's forget the security guard and locker-room business. Okay?"

Confusion washed across Tony's face. "Uh . . . thanks."

"No. Thank you," said Mr. Gore, smiling at Tony.

"You're not going to kill me?"

"Not today. It's been a long time since I've been on a football field. Sometimes I really miss the gridiron. Thanks for bringing me back."

"You're welcome," said Tony, nodding his head. "I had this planned all along. And, uh, by the way, what's a gridiron?"

Mr. Gore chuckled, "Let's watch the game."

The Chiefs scored a touchdown with one second to go in the game. They kicked the extra point and won the game. Chiefs 38, Jets 37.

Seventy-nine thousand fans went bonkers.

Mr. Gore's class got lots of autographs.

Mr. Gore saw many of his old football friends.

Mrs. Hernandez's secretary watched the game on TV and was glad that she wasn't there.

And best of all Tony, Mo, and Anna didn't have to go to the principal's office.

Later that night, after finding out that he was grounded for a week and couldn't watch TV for a month, Tony wrote a letter to David Letterman before he went to bed.

October 31

Dear Mr. Letterman,

My parents are really mad at me. My dad said I went too far today and my mom said I'm teetering on the edge of existence. What does that mean? I thought my teacher would kill me, but he didn't for some strange reason. He actually seemed kind of pleased with me. Anyway here's another top ten list you might want to use on your show.

10. Steal an ice-cream truck and drive to Disney World.

9. Get caught painting a mustache on George Washington at Mount Rushmore.

8. Single-handedly persuade Congress to pass a law making it a federal offense for school cafeterias to serve cold, soggy, limp french fries.

7. Write a best-selling book called *101 Ways to Successfully Avoid Doing Homework*.

6. Organize a nationwide elementary school walkout demanding more and longer recess periods.

5. Chain yourself to a display in Toys "Я" Us and refuse to leave until Geoffrey the Giraffe autographs your hinder.

4. Rollerblade across the United States in your birthday suit.

3. Set a world record for wearing the same pair of underpants the most days in a row.

2. Open the first coffee shop in a school cafeteria and name it Stardorks.

1. Steal the football from an NFL game in progress.

Sincerely,
Tony Baloney

P.S. #1 really happened. Yes, I snatched a football from the Chiefs-Jets game. And all the Chiefs autographed the ball for me! My parents are really mad, though. I'm grounded for a week and can't watch any TV for a month! Call me and I'll explain. My phone number is 816-555-0942. Are you ever going to invite me to be on your show?

The Phone Call

Tony sat at his bedroom desk and doodled on a piece of paper. He was supposed to be doing his homework. Mr. Gore had assigned everybody an essay. Two paragraphs about the football game field trip. One paragraph about the best part of the trip. And the other about the worst part of the trip.

Tony didn't want to write. He didn't want to do anything. He had never been grounded before and didn't like it. No TV for a month, he thought in despair. How will I ever survive? He wadded up the paper he was doodling on and tossed it into his trash can.

The telephone rang. He didn't even try to get

it. It was useless with a teenage sister in the house. Maria always got to the phone first.

"Hey, Baloney. It's for you," Maria yelled from her bedroom.

Tony went into Maria's room. Alternative rock music blared from her stereo. Maria, dressed in her usual clothes—black sneakers, black cargo pants, silver studded black belt, black tank top, and spiked black neck choker—sang into a hairbrush and danced in front of her full-length mirror.

"I'll take it in here," Tony announced, turning the stereo volume down.

"No way, José," said Maria, cranking the volume higher. "Take it in the living room." Then she pushed Tony into the hallway.

"Thanks a lot, Miss MTV," Tony replied. "I didn't want to use your phone, anyway. It's probably full of germs. Teenage germs. The deadliest in the world!"

"You're so immature. Just get out of here and go answer your stupid phone call." Maria rolled her eyes and kicked her door shut.

"Chill out," Tony grumbled as he headed down the hallway to the living room.

* * *

"Hello. This is Anthony Madison," Tony spoke into the phone, wrapping the cord around his hand a couple of times.

"Hello, Anthony. This is David Letterman. But you can call me Dave."

"Yeah. Right. And I'm Bond, James Bond. But you can call me Jim."

"A comedian, folks." A pause. Then: "Really, kid. I'm calling from the *Late Show*."

"Yeah. And I'm talking to you from the moon," Tony replied. "Is this you, Dean?"

"No. This isn't Dean. This is Dave. You know, David Letterman. I host the *Late Show*. And I'm the only guy in New York City who has a space between his front teeth that is wide enough to drive a bus through."

"No way. It's only 4:40. And the *Late Show* doesn't come on until past my bedtime. At 10:30."

"Yes way, kid. We tape the show at 5:30 in the evening. Then we broadcast it later—even past my bedtime. Anyway, my watch shows 5:40. So it's 4:40 in Kansas City."

"I don't believe you. You're Dean's older brother. Aren't you? He put you up to this."

"Listen, kid. I didn't know a Dean when I was pooping my Pampers. I didn't know a Dean when I was the biggest geek in elementary school. I didn't know a Dean when I was Indiana's wackiest weatherman. And I'm telling you I don't know a Dean now. *And* I hope I never know a Dean. As a matter of fact, if I ever meet a Dean, I'll smack him in the head with one of my hams. You've got to believe me. You're speaking to David Letterman."

"Prove it," Tony challenged.

"You got it. Hey, audience. Give a big hello to Anthony."

"HELLO, ANTHONY!"

"Good try, Dean. How many kids do you have in your house?" asked Tony. "I've heard enough. I'm going to hang up now."

"Wait, kid. You can't hang up on the King of Late Night TV. I'd be out of a job if my boss found out that I couldn't keep a defenseless little kid on the phone for a couple of minutes! I'd probably be selling hot dogs on the street corner as early as tomorrow night. Come on. Give me one more try."

"All right," said Tony. "But this better be good. Or I'm out of here."

"Okay. I was watching the Jets-Chiefs game last night. Near the end of the game I see a small bear streak out onto the field and steal the game ball. Then the bear races into the end zone and scores a touchdown. The crowd goes absolutely wild. I say to myself, This is really strange. Bears don't interrupt NFL games in Kansas City. New York—maybe. But not Kansas City. Then later I see an interview on ESPN. And *boom!* It all comes together—the letters I've been getting from Kansas City . . . the top ten lists . . . the cries for help. Then I realize that *you're* the kid who's dying to be on my show. I ain't no dummy, you know. I *do* have my own TV—"

"You *are* David Letterman," Tony interrupted, his heart racing.

"That's right, Anthony."

"You can call me TB. All my friends do."

"You know, TB, you're an instant celebrity. You're all over the TV. You're in the newspapers. You even made the front page of *The New York Times*."

"Really?" Tony asked. "I can't watch TV for a month. I'm grounded. My parents aren't too happy with me."

"Tough luck, TB. But it's true. How would you like to be on the *Late Show*?"

"I'm dreaming," Tony replied. "This isn't really happening."

"Yes, it is, TB. I loved your letters. The top ten lists were hilarious. The bear stunt was fantastic. So, how about it? Are you ready to come to New York?"

"Of course!" Tony exclaimed. "But there's just one thing, Dave."

"What's that?"

"Can I bring my best friends, Mo and Anna? And maybe my teacher?" Tony hesitantly asked.

"You bet, TB. *You're* the famous guy."

"The . . . famous . . . guy," Tony slowly repeated. "I like the way that sounds. You're the best, Dave. Thanks for making my dream come true."

"You earned it, TB. I look forward to having you on the show. Put your mom or dad on the line and I'll have one of my staff members begin making arrangements."

"They're not home right now. They went out to dinner. They made it clear to me that *they* weren't grounded."

"Putting the squeeze on you, eh? Don't worry. We'll call back later. And by the way, who answered the phone?"

"Oh, that was my teenage sister."

"Ah hah. I thought it was Madonna. They must be related."

"Yeah, probably so, Dave."

"Take care, TB. I hope to see you soon."

"You will," Tony said, hanging up the phone. Then he ran down the hall and burst into Maria's room. "Guess what?" he yelled above the blaring music. "David Letterman just called."

"Yeah, right," replied Maria, turning down the volume on her stereo.

"He really did call," insisted Tony. "He wants me to be on his show!"

"Whatever you say, kiddo." Maria put her arm around his shoulders. "You never give up, do you? Let's go to the kitchen and get some ice cream and you can tell me all about it."

"Mom! Dad! Guess what?" Tony said when his parents got home. "David Letterman called while you were gone and invited me to be on the *Late Show*! They're going to call back tonight to talk to you about it."

Mr. and Mrs. Madison took their coats off and hung them in the hallway closet. Mr. Madison looked at Mrs. Madison and rolled his eyes as if to say, "Yeah, right. Here we go again."

Mrs. Madison looked at Tony and said, "Guess what, Tony? While we were at dinner the queen of

England called me on my cell phone and asked me to tea."

Maria wandered into the hallway and joined the conversation. "Guess what, Mom and Dad?" She smiled mischievously and locked eyes with Tony. "*Cosmopolitan* magazine called while you were gone and offered me a job as a supermodel!"

Mr. Madison's eyes twinkled. He smiled at Mrs. Madison and Maria, and then he looked at Tony and said, "You'll never guess who called my cell phone while we were at dinner. Bill Gates called and asked me for some advice about—"

The phone rang and interrupted Mr. Madison.

Maria picked up the phone. "Hello," she said. She listened for a minute and then held out the phone to her dad as a dumbfounded look washed across her face. "It's someone from the *Late Show*. She wants to talk to you."

Tony crossed his arms over his chest, leaned against the wall, smiled, and said, "I told you so."

"Pleeeeeease, Mr. Gore," Tony begged the next morning as he stood next to Mr. Gore's desk. "Will you please take us to the *Late Show*?"

Mr. Gore looked up from the test he was grading. His face hardened and he said, "Do you really think that I have even a slight desire to try to keep tabs on you in New York—one of the busiest cities in the world? Look at the chaos you've caused in Kansas City, TB. I don't even want to *think* about what it would be like to be in New York with you. After all you've put me through. I'd have to have my head examined to even consider such a ridiculous request."

Tony bit his lip and didn't say anything for a few seconds. Then he cautiously said, "I saw something happen to your eyes when you were on the gridiron. They—"

"Gridiron?" interrupted Mr. Gore. "I thought you didn't know what a gridiron was."

"I looked it up in the dictionary."

"Great. Now I have an out-of-control ten-year-old academic begging me to take him to New York," Mr. Gore said as he straightened some papers on his desk.

Tony smiled and shrugged his shoulders. "Really, Mr. Gore. Something weird happened. Your eyes sort of glowed with satisfaction. And you can't deny it."

"Yeah, so what?"

"Well, it happened because part of you belongs on the football field. Right?"

"Maybe, but what does that have to do with me taking you to New York?"

Tony paused and looked away from Mr. Gore. When he looked back his eyes brimmed with tears. "Part of *me* belongs on the *Late Show,* Mr. G. I just know it. I can't explain how I know. But if I could someday step on the stage, and be a part of the *Late Show,* my eyes would glow like yours did."

Mr. Gore stared at Tony for a few seconds, and then his face softened. "You never give up. Do you, TB?" Mr. Gore said, shaking his head with disbelief. "Okay . . . I . . . guess that I'll . . . uh . . . take . . . you."

"You won't regret this, Mr. G!" Tony yelled, throwing his arms around Mr. Gore's neck.

"Actually, I already do," Mr. Gore said as he rolled his eyes and peeled Tony's arms from around his neck.

"I can't wait to tell Anna and Mo," Tony said as he raced toward the classroom door. He stopped, smiled, and said, "Mr. G, I'll have my secretary get you an appointment with a shrink ASAP." Then he disappeared down the hallway.

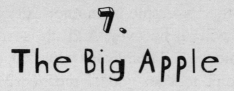

7.

The Big Apple

"Ladies and gentleman, this is your captain speaking," a voice crackled over the intercom system. "I'd like to wish you a happy post-Turkey Day. I can tell you that I had a great one. Ate way too much though." The pilot paused and groaned. "Anyway, do me a favor, would you? If you are presently wandering around this airborne sardine can, would you please return to your seats and buckle up? We're about to hit some nasty air and we may have a heck of a ride for the next few minutes. Sit tight and hopefully you won't lose yesterday's turkey, dressing, cranberries, pumpkin pie, and other assorted goodies. Please don't be alarmed because this won't last long. We'll touch down in the Big Apple in another thirty minutes, and this will all be over. And uh, sorry for the inconvenience and thanks for your cooperation."

"I don't feel so good," moaned Mo as the plane slowly descended through the clouds and lurched as it hit pockets of unstable air. He reached for a barf bag.

"Maybe we'll fly into a portal that leads to another universe," Tony said, plastering his face against the window, "and we'll never be seen again."

"I never should have left Kansas City," Mo whimpered. "I hate flying. Something could happen."

A hand reached through the opening between the two boys' seats and lightly grabbed Mo's shoulder. "It's okay, Mo," Anna said in a soft comforting voice. "You probably won't feel a thing."

Panic filled Mo's eyes. He sat up in his seat, twisted his body, and scanned the airplane cabin. His troubled eyes settled on a curled-up body sprawled out on three seats at the back of the cabin. "Mr. Gore, make them shut up!"

"He can't hear you," Tony said. "He's sleeping like a baby, and he has his MP3 earphones on. Metallica is cranking at full volume, and

Mr. G's probably dreaming about the Chiefs-Jets game."

"Oh, man!" Mo screamed as the plane dropped another thousand feet.

A couple of seconds later the plane resumed its normal flight path. Then a voice crackled over the intercom system again. "This is the captain again. Well, that was quite a ride. Just like a bucking bronco. But I tamed the beast and now we're going to have smooth sailing into LaGuardia. We should touch down in about twenty minutes. Please keep your seat belts buckled . . . just in case."

Mo pulled his face out of the barf bag. His usual rich, chocolate-colored skin had a sickly whitish-brown sheen. His glazed eyes stared through the seat in front of him.

Tony waved his hand back and forth in front of Mo's eyes. "Anybody home? It's all over."

Mo didn't say a word.

"What's wrong with him?" asked Anna.

"I don't know. He looks like a zombie." Tony snapped his fingers in front of Mo's face. "Snap out of it, man."

Mo's eyes gradually refocused on Tony's hand. A weak smile parted his lips. "I sort of lost it there. At least I didn't launch my breakfast."

"Breakfast? That stuff wasn't breakfast. Airlines don't serve food. They serve recycled roach refuse."

Mo groaned again.

"Ladies and gentleman," interrupted the intercom again. "This is your flight attendant speaking. We'll be landing in a few minutes. Please raise your seat backs and tray tables to an upright and locked position. Make sure your seat belts are buckled, and store all loose items safely away under your seat or in the overhead bin. We hope you enjoyed your flight and will fly with us again in the near future."

"I didn't enjoy this flight and I'm never flying again," Mo whined.

"Excuse me," said a flight attendant as she checked the kids' seat belts. She leaned over Tony to take a close look at Mo. "Your friend doesn't look too good. Is he okay?"

"Well, do you mean mentally, or what?"

"I mean is he going to fill up his airsickness bag?"

"You mean barf bag?"

"I mean is he going to be the Archduke of Puke?"

"Hey, you're pretty cool."

"That may be so," answered the flight attendant, "but I couldn't care less whether or not I'm the Princess of Impress. Your friend is my main concern right now. What's his problem?"

"He thinks we're never going to be sent to the principal's office again, and it isn't because we've miraculously become angels. If you know what I mean."

"I know exactly what you mean," said the flight attendant as she reached down and stroked Mo's hair. "Listen, kid. Nothing bad is going to happen. In a few minutes we're going to touch down—safe and sound—and you'll be in one of the most exciting cities in the world. I have to take my seat now. You hang in there and I'll be back to check on you after we've landed. Okay?"

Mo looked up. Relief filled his big brown eyes. "Okay," he murmured. "And thanks."

"You're welcome," the flight attendant replied as she headed toward the back of the plane. "And you three kids make sure your backpacks are under the seat in front of you."

The plane descended some more and lurched when the tires hit the runway. A voice crackled over the intercom system again. "This is the captain. I hope you enjoyed your flight because I certainly did—especially the airborne gymnastics. It's 9:30 A.M. and we're right on schedule. Thanks for flying with us and we hope to see you on another flight. Enjoy the rest of your holiday and your stay in the Big Apple."

8.
Through Rain . . .

"I *don't* like this," Anna said, picking at a button on her shirt. "I've never seen so many people before. Kansas City's airport is nice and calm. This place reminds me of a beehive that's been whacked with a stick."

"We haven't even left the terminal yet! I wonder what it's like out there?" Tony asked as he pointed toward the exit doors. "It's probably worse there than it is in here."

"I'm not so sure I want to be here," said Anna.

"Yeah, what a morning," Mo moaned. "I thought we were goners on our flight *and* I nearly heaved my breakfast. I should have my head examined *and* I should have stayed at home."

"That's called air turbulence, Mo. Nearly heaving is a small price to pay for fame. Don't forget why we're here," Tony replied. "David Letterman. The *Late Show*. The top ten."

"I know, but this is creepy," said Anna, looking at her watch. "It's only 9:45. Maybe we can get a flight back to Kansas—"

"Hmm hmm." Mr. Gore cleared his throat.

All three kids turned and looked at him.

He leaned against a wall with his arms crossed over his huge chest. "Don't forget that I am here, kiddos. Everything is going to be okay." He paused and joined the kids. "LaGuardia is a piece of cake. I've been through this airport many times. We'll be out of here in no time at all. We just need to hook up with our limo driver, and he'll take us to The Michelangelo, where we can grab a shower and relax before—"

"The Michel—what?" interrupted Tony.

"The Michelangelo," said Mr. G. "A charming hotel not too far from the Ed Sullivan Theater. Anyway, before you know it we'll be chatting with David Letterman—"

"Excuse me, sir," interrupted an airport security guard as he walked up to Mr. Gore. "Please step over there with me for a couple of minutes." He motioned to a nearby spot where more security guards were standing.

Mr. Gore glanced at the other guards. "Excuse me?"

"Security check, sir."

"And bring your carry-on bag as well," said the security guard.

"Come on, kids," Mr. Gore said. He didn't look pleased.

"I'm sorry, sir. The children must stay here. They will not be out of sight. We'll be just a few feet away."

"But I'm their chaperone," Mr. Gore protested.

"Now, sir," the security guard said.

"Okay," Mr. Gore said. "Give me one minute."

Mr. Gore corralled the three kids together. "Do *not* leave this spot. For *no* reason. Do you understand?"

"Yeah, sure," Mo said.

"Yes, sir," Anna said.

"No problemo," said Tony. "And don't give them any trouble, Mr. G. You don't want to end up in the slammer."

Mr. Gore rolled his eyes, walked away, and mumbled, "I knew I'd regret this trip, *and* I should have seen a shrink."

The three kids watched as the guard searched through Mr. Gore's bag.

"Mr. G doesn't look too happy," Anna said.

Mo motioned to the right. "Do you hear that? What's that noise?"

A low rumble reverberated through the airport, getting louder and louder, and then a sea of people rounded a corner and rushed down the terminal toward the kids.

"Totally weird," declared Anna.

Tony exclaimed, "That's Alisha Keenan coming toward us! I'm sure of it."

"Yeah, right," said Mo. "No way."

"It is!" squealed Anna, standing on her tiptoes to get a better look. "There must be a million people following her."

"This is cool," said Tony. "First we're going to meet Alisha Keenan and then we're going to meet David Letterman. I wonder who else we'll meet today?"

"With my luck, Barney," replied Mo.

In a matter of seconds the wave of people— Alisha Keenan, bodyguards, paparazzi, television crews, and a throng of screaming fans—engulfed Tony, Anna, and Mo, and swept them toward the exit doors.

"Grab my hands!" Tony hollered.

Anna grabbed Tony's left hand. Mo grabbed Tony's right hand. A split second later, Mr. Gore broke away from the security guard and reached for Mo's free hand. But before he could grab it, the wave of people rushed forward and carried the three kids away.

The wave rushed through the exit doors and crashed into the street. A long white limo was parked by the curbside; its back door open. The street looked like a stormy ocean of people surging back and forth.

The three kids, still holding hands, found themselves caught in the surge. At one moment they were pushed forward, and the next backward. They were tossed about like pieces of driftwood in rough seas.

"We have to get out of this mess and find Mr. Gore," said Tony. "Follow me."

"Okay," said Mo.

Tony pushed through the crowd, with Mo and Anna following close behind.

"Mr. Gore, where are you?" Anna cried.

"Mr. Gore, we're over here!" Mo shouted. "By the. . . ." He frantically looked around for a landmark as his voice died out. There was not one to be seen—just people, concrete walls, windows, piles of snow, and various vehicles.

People yelled. People pushed. Jets roared overhead.

"He probably can't hear us," Tony said above the pandemonium. "It's too crazy out here. Let's just keep going."

Eventually the crowd thinned slightly, and the kids popped out of the sea of people near a taxi stand.

"One minute," said Anna. "My mom gave me her cell phone. I have Mr. Gore's cell number. I'm going to call him and tell him we're okay. He's probably really worried about us."

"Good idea," said Mo.

Anna pulled a cell phone out of her pocket, punched in the numbers, and placed the call. She waited a bit and then hung up the phone. "All I got was that stupid recording saying that his number wasn't available and to call back later. What do we do now?" Anna asked, plopping herself down on the icy street curb. Tears trickled down her cheeks.

"That's a good question," Mo said, plopping himself down on her right side.

"A very good question," Tony said, plopping himself down on her left side.

The three of them silently stared at the confusion around them.

Their reverie was broken by a short, dark-skinned man. "May Raj help you?"

"May who do what?" Tony asked, looking up at the stranger.

"May Raj help you?" The stranger paused and adjusted the white turban on his head. "Tears. Tears on the girl's face. Girl not happy."

"No kidding," Tony replied. "None of us are doing the happy dance right now. All we're doing is freezing our hinders off."

"Happy dance? Hinder?"

"You're not from around here. Are you?"

"No. Raj from Bombay," the stranger said as a big smile creased his face. "Bombay in India. No snow in Bombay."

"Mr. Raj, how can you help us?" Tony asked.

"Raj taxi driver," the stranger proudly replied. "Best taxi driver in New York City. Raj was best child psychologist in Bombay. As soon as Raj gets psychologist license, he will be best child psychologist in New York City."

"That's great and all," replied Mo. "But I don't see how that's going to help us."

"Yeah," agreed Anna, wiping a tear from her cheek.

"Wait a minute," Tony said, hopping to his feet. "Maybe Mr. Raj can take us to the *Late—*"

"Yeah," Mo interrupted. "That's a great idea."

"I don't know," Anna said. "What about Mr. Gore? How will we ever find him?"

"Don't forget that he said he's been to New York a bunch of times. He can take care of himself," said Tony. "And besides, Dave will know how to find him."

"Taxis aren't free, you know."

Tony reached into his pocket and took out a wad of money and waved it in Anna's face. "This should be enough."

"Where did you get that?"

Tony smiled. "I raided my piggy bank."

Mo hopped up. "Way to go, TB. I've got some money, too, so we're in good shape. Let's get out of here."

Tony turned to the taxi driver. "Mr. Raj, can you give us a ride?"

"Of course! And you will be lucky. Lovely girl can tell Raj why she is crying while Raj is driving, and Raj will help her feel better."

Tony reached down, grabbed Anna's hand, and pulled her up.

She brushed the snow off her backside and smiled at the taxi driver. "Let's go, Mr. Fantastic."

He smiled at Anna. "Follow Raj, angel."

He pushed through the crowd of people and the three kids followed closely behind. A couple of minutes later they reached a grimy yellow taxi. He popped the trunk open. "Raj glad to help."

The three kids tossed their backpacks into the trunk and hopped into the backseat.

"Thanks, Mr. Raj," said Tony.

"Raj glad to help," he repeated as he climbed into the front seat and started the engine.

Tony tapped on the Plexiglass barrier between the front seat and the backseat. Raj slid a small window open between the kids and himself.

"Why is this here?" Tony asked, tapping on the Plexiglass again.

"So bad guy can't get Raj."

"Oh, great," said Mo. "Now we have to worry about criminals, too. I knew I should have stayed in Kansas City."

"Raj know Kansas City. In the middle of America. Yes?"

"Yes," said Anna. "It's in the middle of America. That's where we're from."

"Raj from Bombay!"

"Yeah, we know," Tony said. "Is it okay if we leave now?"

"Raj ready. Where you want to go?"

"Can you please take us to Letterman's?"

"No problem."

About an hour later the taxi pulled up in front of a huge building that stretched a full two city blocks. Tony opened the door and climbed out of the taxi. "What?" he said as he stared up at the classical building and read the large words etched above the doorway: NEITHER RAIN NOR SNOW, NOR HEAT NOR GLOOM OF NIGHT STAYS THESE COURIERS FROM THE SWIFT COMPLETION OF THEIR APPOINTED ROUNDS.

9.

King Kong

"Mr. Raj, this is a post office!" Tony exclaimed.

"Raj know," said Raj, nodding his head. "Raj here many times."

"But why did you bring us here?"

"You say you want to go to the letter man. The letter man here. This is the post office. You mail letters here."

"I didn't mean the letter man," Tony said, shaking his head in disbelief. "I meant David Letterman. I asked you to take us to David Letterman."

"Where?"

"Not where? Who!"

"Raj not understand."

"David Letterman is a famous guy. He's got his own television show called the *Late Show with David Letterman*. I wanted you to take us to him."

"Raj not have TV. So Raj not know this man."

Mo climbed out of the car. "I knew I should have stayed in Kansas City."

Anna climbed out of the car. "This trip is a disaster. I want to go home."

The taxi driver lowered his head. "Raj very sorry."

"It's not your fault," Tony said, patting the taxi driver on the shoulder. "I didn't make myself clear enough."

"Raj give you another ride?"

Tony took the wad of money out of his pocket and held it out to the taxi driver. "No, that's okay, Mr. Raj. How much for the ride?"

"Nothing. Raj not take your money."

"Why not?"

"Because driver not take money when make mistake," said Raj, pushing Tony's hand away.

"Thanks. That's really nice of you."

"Yeah," said Mo. "You didn't have to do that."

"Yes Raj did," the taxi driver said, climbing into his car. Then he wrote his telephone number on a piece of paper and handed it to Anna. "Please call Raj if you need any help—to go somewhere or . . . psychological!" He paused, smiled, twirled his forefinger around the side of his head, and winked. "Good luck, kids from Kansas City. I hope you find the letter man."

Anna smiled at the taxi driver. "Thanks, best taxi driver and future best child psychologist in New York City."

"You welcome, angel," Raj said, and then he paused, looked at Tony and Mo, and smiled. "You two devils welcome, too." Then he drove down the street and disappeared into the heavy traffic.

"What now?" asked Mo. "We can't stand in front of the James A. Farley Post Office for the rest of our lives."

"The subway," answered Tony.

"Are you nuts, TB?" Anna said. "We'll get lost."

"No way. It'll be a piece of cake."

"Have you ever ridden a subway?" asked Mo.

"Well . . . uh . . . no, but it can't be that hard. We'll pay. Get on. Ride. Get off."

Mo kicked an empty soda can on the side-walk. It flew into the street and died a sudden death when a delivery truck smashed it beyond recognition. "We'll pay. Get on. Ride. Get off. Get mugged and die just like that soda can. And then someone will find our frozen bodies a day or two later. And we'll be sitting on a cloud watching them cart our bodies away and wish we'd never gone to New York City to be on some stupid TV show in the first place."

"You worry too much, Mo," Tony said as he slid his left arm around Mo's shoulder. "Look around you. We're in the Big Apple. This is the most exciting city in the world, and we're this close to fame and glory." He held his hand in front of Mo's face, thumb and forefinger an inch apart. "We're going to survive to see another day, and we're going to have a great time while we're at it. Trust me."

"Every time I trust you I get into troub—"

Anna thumped both boys' heads. "Hello. I'm here, too. Both of you talk too much. You can stay here and discuss the weather. You can discuss whether or not the Easter bunny is real. You can discuss the difference between boys and girls if you want. I don't really care what you do. I'm freezing my hinder off, so I'm going to find David Letterman by myself." Anna shook her head and walked away from the boys. Within seconds she melted into the crowd of people hurrying up and down the sidewalk.

Tony and Mo looked at each other and smiled.

"Hey, wait up," Tony said. "You don't have to be such a grouch."

"Yeah," added Mo.

The boys zigzagged in and out of people on the busy sidewalk and caught up with Anna.

"What *is* the difference between boys and girls?" asked Mo.

"Nice weather, huh?" asked Tony.

"You guys are impossible," said Anna. "Let's find a subway station. Now."

"Okay," said Tony. "Next stop. The subway station to the Empire State Building. My grandmother ordered tickets on-line and sent them to me. I've got them packed away in my backpack."

"What about the *Late Show*?" asked Anna.

"The show doesn't tape until late this after-noon, so we'll do both. We can't leave the Big Apple without going to the top of the Empire State Building!" He stopped a policeman who was passing by. "Excuse me, sir. But can you please tell us which subway to take to the Empire State Building?"

The policeman took a bite of celery smeared with peanut butter. "You don't need to take the subway, kid. Walk it in ten. Go up to Thirty-fourth Street, hang a right. It'll be about three blocks down on your right."

"We're that close?" asked Tony.

"That's right," said the policeman, stuffing the rest of the celery in his mouth, and then wiping peanut butter from his lips with the back of his hand. "I gotta get to the precinct. See you around."

"Thanks, sir."

"No problem, kid."

"Let's go," said Tony.

"Hey, wait a minute," Anna said. "I better call Mr. Gore again." She dialed, then groaned. "Same recording."

"Well, then," said Tony, "let's head to the Empire State Building."

About five minutes later the kids stood at the corner of Thirty-fourth Street and Broadway. They stared up at the sky. They were speechless.

Finally Tony broke the silence. "How in the world did King Kong climb up that baby?"

10.
Die Hard

"I *hate* elevators more than airplanes," said Mo as the doors slid shut. "At least airplanes have pilots."

"This thing does have a pilot. Me!" Tony proclaimed as he pushed a button with the number eighty highlighted on it (which happened to be the highest number on the button panel). "I don't know what you're so worried about. What's the big deal? We're going up eighty floors. So what?"

"Yeah," added Anna. "It'll only take a couple of minutes to get there."

"I'm worried about two things. How come no one collected our tickets *before* we got in the elevator? *And* TB could do a lot of damage in a couple of minutes."

Tony smiled. "Mo, Mo, Mo. How could you say

that about me? I'm just an innocent kid from Kansas City heading to the top of the Empire State Building. And what's the big deal about the tickets? They'll probably collect them when we get to the top."

"Innocent? Yeah, right," said Mo, shaking his head. "Something always *happens* when you're around."

"This is what's *happening*: We're already at the nineteenth floor," said Tony, pointing at the floor indicator lights above the sliding doors.

"No, this is what's *happening*: I've got to go."

"Go? That's what we're doing. We're going up, Mo."

"No, man. I've got to *go*!" said Mo, crossing his legs. "I told you I needed to make a pit stop in the lobby. But, no, *we* couldn't stop because you rushed into the nearest elevator and ignored the fact that I needed a rest room, not an elevator. Whenever you're on one of your *missions* nothing else matters, does it?"

Tony shrugged his shoulders. "Sorry about that. You can hit the urination station in a little bit. We're already halfway there."

The three kids stared at the lights blinking one by one as the elevator moved up the shaft: 41–42–43–44–45 . . .

"I'll never make it. I'm going to explode," said Mo as he shuffled his feet and wiggled his legs.

"Nice moves, Mo," said Anna, bobbing her head to imaginary music. "You're pretty good at the 'Toilet Tango.'"

Mo ignored Anna and stared at the blinking lights above the elevator doors: 74–75–76–77 . . .

"I wonder what would happen if I pushed this red button?" Tony asked as he pushed a red emergency button on the elevator button panel.

Somewhere between floors 78 and 79 the elevator lurched to a stop and bounced up and down like it was on the tail end of a bungee jump cord; the lights flickered on and off for a few seconds, and then went completely out.

"I guess that's what happens!" Tony proudly proclaimed.

"I'm never leaving Kansas City again," moaned Mo as he slid to the floor and crossed his legs. "This is not good."

"What are we going to do now?" asked Anna with a hint of alarm in her voice. "This is worse than not good. It's sort of scary."

"I have a small flashlight in my backpack," said Tony, hoisting his backpack off his shoulders. "My mom made me pack it in case of an emergency."

He rooted around in his backpack until he found the flashlight. "Let there be light," he said, switching the flashlight on. He shined the flashlight on Mo and found him crouched in a corner with his hands where they shouldn't be.

He shined the flashlight on Anna and found her leaning against the wall with fear written on her face. "We need to do something," she croaked. "I'm starting to get really scared."

"Actually, as far as I'm concerned, fear is not my major concern right now. We need to do something," Mo said, clenching his teeth, "or I'm going to flood this elevator. I can't hold it much longer."

Tony shined the flashlight on the wall and found a telephone. He picked the phone up and put it to his ear. "Nothing." He hung it up.

"Great," said Mo.

"I've got an idea, Anna," Tony said, handing the flashlight to Anna. "Shine the light on my belly." Tony unlatched his belt, took it off, held it out, and the buckle glinted in the light.

"This is nuts. What exactly are you going to do with a belt?" asked Mo, continuing to squirm in the corner.

"Save the day. Just like Bruce Willis did when he got stuck in an elevator in an old movie called

Die Hard. He was battling some nasty terrorists in the movie. It was pretty cool. Did you ever see it?"

"Yeah," said Anna. "I like Bruce Willis. He's handsome."

"Disgusting," groaned Mo. "You better save the day—now! Or we might be the first people to *drown* in an elevator in the history of the Empire State Building."

"Anna, would you please shine the flashlight on the door?" asked Tony.

"Sure," said Anna, shining the light on the door.

Tony slid the belt buckle into the crack where the two elevator doors met. Then he pried the doors open an inch or two. A beam of light penetrated the dark elevator. He slid his fingers into the crack, wrapped them around the edge of one door, and pulled as hard as he could. He forced the door to slide open a couple of more inches. Then he stuck his foot in the gap to prevent the door from closing and continued to pull until he was able to wriggle his body into the gap. Finally, he put his back against the edge of one door and a foot on the edge of the other door, pushed with his back, and slid the doors open enough for a body to slither through. Light flooded the elevator. "What do you see, Anna?"

"A floor. At eye level."

"Good. Now we just need to climb out of this baby."

"I'll go first," said Mo. "Then I'll pull both of you up."

Mo tossed his backpack up onto the floor, placed a foot on Tony's knee, and grabbed the edge of the floor with both hands. "Here goes," he said, pushing and pulling himself up onto the floor. "I made it!"

"Good," said Anna.

Mo lay on his front side and stuck his head down into the elevator. "You're next, Anna."

"Hurry," said Tony, gritting his teeth. "I don't think I can hold this open much longer."

Anna tossed Tony's backpack up to Mo. Then she tossed hers. She placed a foot on Tony's knee and grabbed Mo's hands. "Pull, Mo!" A couple of seconds later she wriggled through the opening and joined Mo.

"We've got a problem here, TB," said Mo. "If I try to pull you up, the doors will close on you. So I'm going to hold the doors open, and Anna can pull you up."

"Just shut up and do it. Now!"

Mo propped open the door for Tony. Anna lay

on her front side, threaded her arms through the opening between Mo's legs and the edge of the floor, and stuck her hands into the elevator. "Now," said Mo.

Tony reached up and grabbed Anna's hands. "Pull!" A couple of seconds later he wriggled through Mo's legs and collapsed onto the floor beside Anna. The elevator doors slid shut.

Mo read a sign on the wall and then looked down at Tony and Anna. "Welcome to the seventy-ninth floor of the Empire State Building."

Anna rolled over and kissed Tony on the cheek. "Thanks for saving the day. You're better than Bruce Willis any old day."

Tony's face turned red and he smiled. "Gee, thanks."

Mo rolled his eyes, shook his head, and gazed down the hallway. "If you two lovebirds will excuse me, I need to take care of some business."

At that moment four guys wearing black uniforms, black helmets, and black bulletproof vests rushed around a corner of the hallway and headed directly for the kids.

"Don't move!" one of them yelled.

Another guy yelled, "All of you stay where you are, and place your hands behind your heads!"

"Now I *am* scared," Anna whined.

"I guess your *business* will have to wait," said Tony as he placed his hands behind his head. "I don't think these guys are going to let you go any-where."

"If these guys don't kill you," Mo moaned, "*I* will."

The four guys stopped about ten feet from the elevator. Then one of them said, "They're *kids*! What's going on here? I don't think there's a real security breach here."

Tony said, "Excuse me, sir, we're *tour*ists, not *terror*ists. The only person I terrorize is my teacher! We just want to go to the top of the Empire State Building."

"Not so," Mo whined. "I want to go some-where else."

Anna started crying. "Please don't arrest us. We just got stuck on an elevator. That's all. We didn't do anything wrong."

The leader spoke into a small microphone clipped onto his shirt collar: "There seems to be a problem here. The suspects are kids. What do you want us to do?" He listened for a couple of minutes through a small earphone stuck in his ear.

"Stand down, men," he said to the three guys with him. "There's been a mess up here."

"The only mess up here," moaned Mo, "is TB, his finger, and a stupid red button in the elevator."

The four men walked over to the kids and helped them up. "Sorry, kids. The building's security computer system reported suspicious activity on your elevator. And these days you can't be too careful. I'm really sorry that this happened. Someone from the Empire State Building Public Relations Department will be here in a few minutes to discuss your situation with you."

"No problemo, sir," said Tony as he took a camera out of his backpack. "Can we get our picture taken with you guys? Our friends at school will think it's really cool that we were almost busted by a SWAT team."

"No problem, kid," replied the leader. "We'll get the public relations pers—"

"No problemo!" interrupted Mo. "I'm sorry to report that there *is* a problem here! You seem like nice guys, and I'd love to share a memorable Kodak moment with you, but I have *serious* business to take care of." Then Mo took off and rocketed down the hall. He flew into a room with a symbol of a man painted on the door.

11.
East Village

"I can't believe that there are seventy-three elevators in the Empire State Building and the one we get on is not for *tourists,* but for *tenants, and* when we stopped it we were nearly arrested," said Tony as they exited the building. "And we never even made it all the way to the top."

"Yeah, it stinks," said Anna, "that kids have to be with an adult to go to the observation deck. But maybe Mr. G can take us later. We still have the tickets."

"The top? Who cares? At least we made it out of there alive, and I didn't explode and flood the whole building," said Mo. He paused and sniffed the air. "Hey, what's that smell?"

Tony pointed to a vendor cart on the sidewalk. "Street hot dogs, my man. I'm starving. Let's get a dog."

"Sounds good," said Anna.

Mo looked at his watch. "It's lunchtime, count me in."

The kids walked over to the vendor and placed their orders.

"Thank you," said Tony, taking his order from the hot-dog guy. "We need to get to the *Late Show*. What subway should we take?"

"Go down to Thirty-fourth and Sixth and take the R uptown—three stops—to Fifty-seventh Street," said the hot-dog guy, handing Anna her order. "Then walk a couple of blocks over to Broadway and West Fifty-third Street. You'll see the Ed Sullivan Theater. You can't miss it."

"Did you two get that?" asked Tony.

"Get what?" said Mo, taking his order from the hot-dog guy.

Anna jammed half of her hot dog into her mouth. "Yeah, sure," she mumbled.

"Never mind. I'll remember," said Tony.

"I'm going to try to call Mr. G again," said Anna. "He must be worried sick about us."

Anna dialed the number, listened for a bit, and then hung up. "I got that stupid recording again. I wonder if something's wrong with his cell phone?"

"Maybe," said Mo, "but there's nothing we can do about it now. So let's go find Dave."

"Yeah, let's do it," said Tony.

The kids stood at the subway entrance.

"I guess this is it," said Tony. "Let's go."

They descended into the gloom of the subway, bought their Metrocards, pushed through the turnstile, and waited for the train. A few minutes later the ground rumbled and a strong wind whooshed through the waiting area.

A train rushed into the station and screeched to a halt. The doors slid open, and people surged on and off the train.

"What train did the hot-dog guy tell us to take?" asked Tony. "This is the F train."

Anna shrugged her shoulders. "Let's take this one. It probably doesn't matter."

The kids hopped onto the crowded train.

"I guess it's standing room only," said Anna, grabbing a pole.

"What stop did the hot-dog guy say?" asked Tony, grabbing Anna's backpack to steady himself as the train took off.

"The fourth? No, the fifth?" said Mo as he grabbed a pole. "Do these things ever crash?"

Tony thumped his forehead with the heel of his hand. "Please, give it a rest. Will you?"

The train thundered through the tunnel and screeched to a halt. People got off. People got on. "Stop number one," said Anna as the train took off again.

The train rumbled for a few minutes through the tunnel and screeched to a halt. People got off. People got on. "Stop number two," said Mo, letting go of the pole to adjust the straps of his backpack. The train lurched forward causing him to lose his balance. Then someone bumped into him and he fell to his knees. A hand reached down, grabbed his, and pulled him up. The girl had skin the color of chocolate and vanilla mixed together. Long silky black hair cascaded around her pretty face. Her big brown eyes sparkled with mischief.

She smiled at Mo and held up his stocking cap. "Sorry about that. I think you dropped this," she said as she stuffed the cap into his coat pocket.

Mo's face turned reddish. "Uh . . . that's okay," he said as he looked down and kicked a pole with the toe of his shoe. "It wasn't your fau—"

"Look at that," Tony interrupted as he elbowed Mo in the ribs. "There's a pigeon in this car."

Mo looked down. "TB, you're telling the truth for once!"

"He's so cute," said Anna. "I wonder how he got on the subway?"

"He thinks he's a passenger," Tony said, reaching toward the pigeon. "Do you have a Metrocard, little guy?"

Just as Tony was attempting to pet the pigeon's head, the train pitched and Tony lost his balance; he frantically flailed his arms to keep upright. As he was windmilling his arms, one of his hands lightly whacked the pigeon's head. The pigeon panicked and launched himself into flight. He wildly beat his wings as he bounced around the subway car like a steel ball rocketing around a pinball machine. People ducked. People screamed. People pushed and shoved. After a couple of erratic loops around the car, the pigeon stopped his flight in midair and made an emergency landing on Mo's head. The pigeon flapped his wings a couple of times and then folded them next to his body.

Then Mo flapped his arms wildly as if he was going to launch *himself* into flight. "Help! Get this thing off me! He's going to kill me!"

A little old lady stepped forward and pushed Mo's arms to his side. "He wouldn't kill you, sonny, but he did poop on you," she said as she lightly cupped her hands around the pigeon and pulled him off Mo's head. Then she cooed at the pigeon. "I'll let you go at my stop, you poor little thing."

Mo surveyed the pigeon damage. "Disgusting."

The train screeched to a halt.

"Stop number five," said Tony as he grabbed Mo's jacket collar and tugged on it. "This is where we get off."

The doors slid open and the kids joined the stream of people that surged off the train. A minute later they popped out of the subway station.

Mo took a tissue out of his coat pocket and wiped off the poop. "Totally gross. I'm never riding the subway again. Actually, I'm never going to come to this city again. This isn't the Big Apple; this is the Rotten Apple."

"Chill, Mo. A little bird doo never hurt anyone. So . . . where to now?" asked Tony, pointing at a sign. "We're at Houston and Second."

"We're supposed to walk somewhere over to somewhere and then we'll be there," said Anna. "Remember?"

"Whatever," mumbled Tony as a puzzled

expression blanketed his face. "This just doesn't seem right."

The girl with the big brown eyes popped out of the subway station, detoured around the kids, and headed down the sidewalk. She stopped, turned around, and smiled at Mo. Then she turned and headed back down the sidewalk.

"The *Late Show* is that way," said Mo, nodding his head in the direction of the girl.

A taxi zoomed past. The driver honked, swerved to the side of the road, hit his brakes, and screeched to a halt. He put his car in reverse, backed up to the kids, and rolled his window down. "Hello, kids from Kansas City! Raj surprised to see you again!"

"Hi, Mr. Raj! We're surprised to see you, too!" exclaimed Tony.

"What you doing all the way over here?" Raj asked.

"We're still looking for David Letterman," answered Mo.

"You not find the letter man yet? You need ride?"

"No, thanks. We're just a couple of blocks away," said Tony, nodding his head to the right, "so we can walk."

Raj looked at Anna and concern washed over his face. "Tears all gone now, angel? You better now?"

"Yes, Mr. Raj," Anna answered with a big smile. "Thanks for asking."

"You still have Raj's phone number?"

"Yes, I do," said Anna, patting her coat pocket. "Right here."

"Good! Remember, you call Raj anytime and I come help you. Okay?" Raj said.

"We will. I promise," said Anna.

"Okay, then. Best taxi driver in New York City go back to work now. Be safe, kids from Kansas City," said Raj. He put his car in gear, pulled into the traffic, and joined the flow of cars rushing down the street.

"Amazing. I can't believe we saw him again," said Anna.

"Yeah, it is amazing," agreed Mo as he looked down the street in the direction that the girl went. "So . . . what now?"

Tony shrugged his shoulders. "What do you think, Anna?"

Anna shrugged her shoulders. "Who knows? Maybe Mo's right about the *Late Show*."

"Could be. Let's go."

The three kids took off down the sidewalk. They passed a sign attached to the side of a building that read: EAT AT HAVELI'S. STRAIGHT AHEAD. 100 SECOND AVENUE. THE BEST RESTAURANT IN THE EAST VILLAGE.

12.
The Big Problem

After a couple of blocks Anna stopped and looked left and right. "The hot-dog guy said we're supposed to walk somewhere over to somewhere and then we'll be there. As far as I'm concerned, we've walked somewhere over to somewhere and now I say we go right and then we'll probably be there. What do you think?"

"Whatever," mumbled Mo.

"I think," said Tony, "that you should give me your cell phone, Anna, and *I'll* try to call Mr. G. Maybe I'll have better luck reaching him than you."

Anna gave the phone to Tony. Tony dialed the number, cocked his head, and held the phone to his ear. After a few seconds he shook his head back and forth and said, "My luck stinks, too."

"Not just your luck," Mo said, pinching his nose. "Do you know what this spells? D-E-O-D-O-R-A-N-T?"

Tony ignored Mo. "I got the stupid no-reception recording, too, Anna. I think that cell companies *and* boys with really long names that are impossible to spell S-T-I-N-K," he said as he looked at Mo. "And I also think that you are *right,* Anna, so *right* it is. Pretty funny, huh? *Right* and *right*?"

"Yeah, it was so funny that you should have your own late night television show," Mo sarcastically replied.

Tony thumped Mo on the shoulder and smiled. "I will have my own show someday, my stinky friend, but first things first," Tony said, stepping ahead of Anna and Mo and taking the lead. "David Letterman, here we come!"

The three kids turned right onto Third Street and plodded down the sidewalk.

Tony stopped abruptly; Anna and Mo ran into the back of him.

"What are you doing?" asked Mo.

"Check it out," said Tony. "I think maybe we've

walked somewhere over to somewhere to the . . . uh . . . wrong place."

"Wow!" exclaimed Mo. "Look at all of the motorcycles. There must be fifty of them."

"Choppers. Not motorcycles," said Anna.

The chrome motorcycles—lined up in a perfect row—gleamed in the bright sunlight. Tony walked up to the first motorcycle. "What a beauty," he said, lightly stroking the smooth, black leather seat. Then he cocked his head to the side and smiled at Mo.

"No," said Mo. "You're not going to do it."

Tony slung his leg over the seat and slid onto the motorcycle. He grabbed the handlebar grips. "I wonder if my mom would let me have one of these?"

Anna slid onto the second motorcycle. She flipped her hair over her shoulder and grabbed the handlebar grips. "Anna the Biker Chick . . . much better than Anna Banana."

Mo looked at Anna; then he looked at Tony. "I should have my head examined," he said as he slung his leg over the third motorcycle.

Immediately a shrill alarm sounded from the motorcycle. Mo's eyes seemed to expand to the size of tennis balls. "Ahhhhhh!" he screamed, launching himself toward Anna's motorcycle, and tumbling to the pavement. As he fell, his foot briefly caught on the motorcycle, causing it to teeter back and forth and then slowly fall to the right. It slammed into the next motorcycle, causing it to slam into the next motorcycle. Within seconds, a chain reaction of motorcycle dominoes crashed down the length of choppers that lined the street. Numerous alarms blared by the time the last motorcycle toppled to the pavement.

Tony and Anna sat on their motorcycles and quietly stared at the debacle. For once in his life, Tony was speechless. Mo slowly stood up, brushed the snowy grime from his pants, and gawked with disbelief.

A couple of seconds later, Tony looked into the rearview mirror of his motorcycle. "Uh, oh!" he yelled. "Anna! Mo! We may have a problem—a *big* problem."

The big problem casually leaned against a door and slowly tapped the toe of one of his black motorcycle boots on the sidewalk—up and down, up and down, up and down. His faded blue jeans looked like they were at least a hundred years old. A long ponytail hung over the back of his sleeveless black T-shirt, and a gold hoop dangled from his left earlobe. Mirrored sunglasses sat on his crooked nose, and a scraggly beard lay over his bulging belly, almost reaching to his big silver belt buckle.

"Uh, aren't you kind of cold?" yelled Tony.

The big problem didn't say a word. He just crossed his huge tattooed arms over his ample belly and eyeballed the kids.

He stared at them.

They stared at him.

He said nothing.

They said nothing.

He took four or five steps toward the kids and stopped. The door opened, and a gang of men and women dressed in black leather poured out of the building. They stopped just behind the big problem and fanned out beside him like a flock of geese. Several of them pulled remote controls out of their pockets and turned off the blaring motorcycle alarms. An eerie silence blanketed the city block.

An eternity seemed to pass before the big problem grumbled in a sort of grizzly bear voice wrapped up in a southern drawl: "Congratulations! You kids just wrecked property that belongs to the Hell's Angels."

"Hell's what?" asked Mo.

"They're the biggest motorcycle gang in the world," said Anna as she slid from her motorcycle. "I think we have a big problem."

Anna, Tony, and Mo moved together.

The gang stared at the kids.

The kids stared at the gang.

The gang said nothing.

The kids said nothing.

The gang slowly moved toward the kids.

"Mo, we really *are* dead now," said Tony as the gang closed the gap between life and death.

13.
The Showdown

Before the gang reached them, Mo lost touch with reality and launched himself at the big problem. He raised his fists and shouted, "I've had a really bad day, mister. I nearly hurled on my flight this morning. I almost got trampled in an Alisha Keenan stampede. I almost experienced urination detonation in the Empire State Building. And a pigeon attacked me on the subway. So back off because I've had about all I can take." He paused and took a breath. "And I'm not going to let some biker dudes end my life or my friends' lives, either. Got that?"

"Calm down, sonny boy," said the big problem as he grabbed Mo's wrists and lowered them.

"Nothin' is gonna to happen to you. My friends and I just finished havin' a meetin' and we're leavin'." He paused and surveyed the toppled motorcycles. "If it's possible to do so."

"Just a meeting?" asked Mo.

"That's right. This is the official headquarters of our New York chapter. We just had a meetin' to figure out how to raise money for the homeless." He looked at Anna and smiled. "So . . . we're a *big* problem, honey?"

Anna looked down and kicked at the sidewalk with the toe of her shoe. Then she glanced at the motorcycle mess. "Sorry, mister. Maybe the three of *us* are the big problem."

"That's okay, honey." He patted Anna on the head. "Accidents are a part of everyday life." He paused, stroked his beard, and smiled with relish. "And I have to admit that I've caused my fair share of catastrophes in my life. Anyway, enough of this mister nonsense. My name's Harley Patrick Davidsun. But my students back home call me Mr. D."

"Students?" asked Tony. "Yeah, right."

"That's right. Kids about your age."

"No way," said Tony.

"Yes way. I'm a fourth-grade teacher."

"Extreme," said Anna, holding out her hand. "My name's Anna. Glad to meet you, Mr. D."

"My pleasure," said Mr. D as he shook Anna's hand.

Mo held out his hand. "My name's Mo." He paused and pointed over his shoulder with his thumb. "And . . . uh . . . sorry about that."

"Glad to meet you, Mo," said Mr. D as he shook Mo's hand. "And don't worry about the cycle carnage; that's what insurance is for."

Tony held out his hand. "My name's Tony. I'm sorry for starting this whole mess. I just couldn't resist."

"No problem, Tony," said Mr. D as he shook Tony's hand. "The cycles are real beauties. I understand one hundred percent."

Tony cleared his throat. "Uh, Mr. D? This may be none of my business, but aren't you a little cold?"

"Dang right, Tony. And if I ain't careful I'm gonna freeze my hinder off."

The three kids looked at one another and smiled.

The door opened and an attractive woman with blonde hair stepped out onto the sidewalk. She pushed her way through the gang and held up a large, black leather jacket. "Harley, did you forget something?"

"I guess I did," said Mr. D, taking the jacket from the woman. "Thanks."

"You're welc—" she paused when the motorcycle mess caught her eye. "What happened?"

"I'll explain later," Mr. D said as a slight smile creased his face.

"An interesting explanation, I'm sure," she said, running her fingers through her hair. "Thanks for the preliminary interview, Harley. We'll do the live interview in an hour at the studio. Okay?"

"I wouldn't miss it," said Mr. D, wiggling into his jacket.

Tony looked at the woman. "Excuse me, ma'am. You look familiar. Do I know you?"

"You might have seen me on the tube. I work at MTV. I just finished talking to Harley about his band's upcoming charity concert."

Tony looked at Mr. D. "Band? Concert? I thought you were a teacher."

Mr. D smiled and shrugged his shoulders. "I guess I'm a rockin' teacher. Kids are my passion and rock is my love."

"Well, the underground New York rock scene passionately loves Harley and the Angels," interrupted the woman, turning her attention to Tony. "You look familiar, too." She stared at Tony for a minute and a smile slowly crept across her face. "I've got it. You're the Kid in the Bear Suit from Kansas City. Aren't you?"

"Yeah," said Tony. "But it's not a big deal."

"Yes, it was! The whole thing was hilarious. I saw every second of it. The chase. The touchdown. The ESPN interview. You were great." The woman held out her hand. "My name's Luca."

Tony shook her hand. "My name's Tony and these are my best friends, Anna and Mo."

"I remember you two as well." Luca paused and shook hands with Anna and Mo. "I have an idea. I'm on the air in an hour for a brief *MTV News* segment about the Angels. Do you kids want to go uptown to the studio and meet some cool people and crash my live interview with Harley?"

"Uptown? I thought we were already uptown," said Tony.

"No, you're downtown."

"Really?"

"Really. So what do you say? Shall we head uptown? How about five minutes of fame?"

"Sure," Tony said hesitantly. "As long as it

doesn't take too long. We have to be somewhere important later this afternoon."

"It won't take long. I promise. My segment is only five minutes."

"Okay," said Tony. "Why not?"

"Great," said Luca. "By the way, what are you kids doing in New York?"

Tony looked at Anna and Mo. "Well, we're here to make a guest appearance on the *Late Show with David Letterman*."

"Yeah, right," said Luca. "And I'm going to shoot an MTV special about the hip-hop scene on Mars."

"Really," said Tony. "We're traveling with Mr. G. He's our teacher, but we like him, anyway."

"Uh huh," said Luca with a hint of disbelief in her voice. "So . . . where is this Mr. G?"

"We sort of got separated from him at the airport this morning and we've been trying to get to the *Late Show* on our ow—"

"I have his cell number," interrupted Anna. "We've tried to call him several times, but we haven't been able to get through. Can you please try to call him?"

"Sure," said Luca as she pulled a cell phone out of her coat pocket. "I should probably give him a call and see if it's okay if I take you kids to the studio. And I can also check on this *Late Show* business."

Anna handed Luca the numbers. Luca dialed the numbers and held the phone to her ear. She waited for a bit and then canceled the call. "Maybe his service doesn't work on the East Coast?"

"Tony's telling the truth," said Anna as she chewed on her lower lip. "Really."

"This time," added Mo.

Luca's eyes darted to the kids and she briefly locked eyes with each of them. A smile slowly spread across her face and she said, "I believe you. When I consider the bear suit business it does make sense for Letterman to invite you to appear on the *Late Show*."

"Thanks," said Anna.

"Under the circumstances, I should probably call one of your parents, since I can't get in touch with your teacher," said Luca.

"Great idea. My mom's probably at home. Let's give her a call," said Tony.

Tony told Luca his telephone number and she punched the keypad, then handed the phone to Tony. "Hi, Mom." Pause. "Yeah, everything's okay. We're out looking at the sights and we're having a great time." Pause. "Yeah, Anna and Mo are here with me." Pause. "Yeah, he's okay, too. I'm not quite sure where he is right now, but he's around—somewhere. Maybe at the urination station." Pause. "Guess what? MTV wants to interview us. Cool, huh? Is it okay with you?" Pause. "Great! Here, would you tell them it's okay?" Tony paused and handed the phone to Luca.

"Hello, my name's Luca Stankovic. I'm a reporter for MTV." Pause. "I'm pleased to speak to you, too, Mrs. Madison. Do you mind if I interview the kids at the studio? We'd love to have the Kid in a Bear Suit and his friends on the air. He's quite a sensation, you know." Pause. "It'll be a live broadcast in about an hour." Pause. "Thanks a lot. And, yes, I'll let him know as soon as possible. Here's Tony." Luca paused and handed the phone back to Tony.

"Thanks, Mom. You're the best." Pause. "I love you, too. Don't forget to turn the channel to MTV. Okay?" Pause. "Good-bye."

Tony handed the phone to Luca. "I've got a nice mom, huh?"

"Yes, you do. She gave me permission to do the interview, but we need to tell a Mr. Gore what's going on as soon as possible."

"Maybe you can call our hotel and leave him a message," said Tony. "We're staying at some hotel called The Michel—something."

"The Michelangelo?" asked Luca.

"Yeah, that's it."

Luca raised her eyebrows. "Nice place. I'll leave a message for him as soon as we get to the studio. And I'll try to call the *Late Show,* too."

"Thanks," said Tony. "Do you think you could take us to the *Late Show* after the interview, too?"

"Sure, it's just up Broadway. We should probably leave now. My driver is waiting for me across the street."

Tony turned to Mr. D. "Thanks for being cool about the cycle business."

"No problem," said Mr. D, reaching into his coat pocket and pulling out a postcard and some tickets. "Here's a postcard with a photo of my band and our website address. You can contact me through the website. And here are four tickets to *The Phantom of the Opera.* Some woman gave them to me at one of our concerts. I've already seen *Phantom.* Go check it out; it'll knock your socks off."

"Thanks so much," said Anna. "I've always wanted to go to a real play."

Mo turned to Mr. D. "Thanks for not *killing* us!"

"You're welcome," said Mr. D, reaching into his coat pocket again and pulling out a key chain. "Here's an official Hell's Angels key chain. When you tell your story back home about your showdown with the Hell's Angels and your friends don't believe you, whip out your key chain as evidence."

"Thanks," said Mo. "I'll put my house key on it."

"We should probably hit the road and grab a quick bite before the interview," said Mr. D, motioning to the other bikers.

Mr. D shook hands with each of the kids and gave Luca a kiss on the cheek. He and his biker friends went over to their toppled cycles. A couple of bikers exchanged heated words with Mr. D. Words like *accident* and *filing* and *insurance* and *don't be idiots* pierced the chilly air. Finally, Mr. D and the bikers righted and mounted their cycles, fired up the engines, and roared off down the street.

"Wow," said Tony. "That was cool. They were cool. He was cool!"

"We really need to get to the studio," said Luca.

"Good idea," said Mo, pulling his stocking cap out of his coat pocket. "Is it always this cold here?"

"No," answered Luca, bending over and picking up a business card that dropped out of Mo's pocket. She handed the card to him as the four of them crossed the street to the waiting MTV car. "Here, you dropped this."

Mo read the card and smiled. Then he handed it to Tony.

Tony read the card, shook his head, and handed it to Anna.

Anna read the card and handed it back to Mo. "How romantic," said Anna.

The following was printed on the front of the card in elegant gold letters: HAVELI'S. THE BEST RESTAURANT IN THE EAST VILLAGE. 100 SECOND AVENUE. TELEPHONE: 212-555-0533.

The following was scrawled on the back of the card in blue ink: DIVYA BARUAH. *divya@haveli. com*. 212-555-0533.

"Did I ever tell you how much I love New York City?" asked Mo as the four of them climbed into the car. "I can't wait to see what else happens today."

Anna smiled and winked at Mo. Tony rolled his eyes and stuck his finger down his throat and gagged. And Mo read the card again.

14.
Giant Sewer Rats, Detours, Toilets, Tattoos, Rock Stars, and Celebrities

"Luca, did you call the hotel or the *Late Show* yet?" Anna asked as Luca rushed past her. "We should try to get in touch with Mr. G."

"Not yet, Anna," Luca answered as she bustled around the set that was buzzing with production and tech crew. "I haven't had time yet. It's always nuts around here before I go on live. I'll call as soon as we're off the air. Okay?"

"Okay," said Anna.

"You're on in two minutes, Luca," a guy from the production crew announced. "Please clear the set."

Bodies immediately vanished and the set became quiet.

"Anna, please go stand with Tony and Mo," Luca said, pointing to the side of the set. "You three will be on after Harley."

"Sure," said Anna.

"And, Harley, please come and take a seat next to me," Luca said as she sat in the second of three plush armchairs.

"Thirty seconds," the production guy announced. When the seconds ticked down to ten, the production guy held up his hands and began a countdown from ten to one with his fingers. When his last finger curled down, he nodded at Luca and an ON THE AIR sign, hanging on the set wall, flashed on.

"This is Luca Stankovic reporting live for *MTV News* from our studio in New York City. Sitting next to me is Harley Patrick Davidsun, lead singer of Harley and the Angels. He and I will talk about the impact his band is making on the underground rock scene and charity causes in New York City. We'll also talk about the impact Harley has on children." Luca paused and smiled at Mr. Davidsun. "Believe it or not, in addition to being a rocker, he's also a fourth-grade teacher. So, Harley . . ."

Tony lightly elbowed Mo and whispered, "Are you ready to see some fireworks?"

"What are you talking about?" Mo whispered as dread filled his eyes.

Tony arched his eyebrows and smiled. "Let's just say that my interview will be . . . interesting."

"For you, maybe," whispered Mo, "but probably not for anyone else."

"I guarantee that this will be a day to remember in MTV history."

"And I guarantee that I am *never* going anywhere with you again."

"Be quiet. This is a no-talking zone, and," whispered Anna, pointing at Luca, "she's about done with Mr. Davidsun."

". . . Harley," Luca said, holding out her hand, "I'd like to end our interview by saying: Keep on teaching . . . and keep on rocking."

"I will," said Mr. Davidsun as he beamed a large smile at Luca and shook hands with her, "because I'm the rockin' teacher."

Luca looked to the side of the set and winked at Tony. "And now I'd like to introduce the worldwide MTV audience to a surprise guest that is full of . . . well . . . surprises. It is my pleasure to introd—"

At that moment the lights went out, bathing the set in total darkness, and alternative rock music blared out of massive speakers. Tony rushed onto the set, hopped onto the empty chair, and stood on it, facing the cameras. The instrumental introduction blared for about twenty seconds, reached a crescendo, and then when the vocals kicked in, colored and laser lights flashed on, and a fog machine pumped fog onto the set. Tony leaped off the chair, landed on his feet, and began aggressively playing an imaginary air guitar. A spotlight focused on him as he bounced around the set miming the words to the rock song.

Luca sat dumbfounded as she watched her interview turn into a simulated rock concert. Mr. Davidsun's head rapidly bobbed up and down, and then he jumped up, grabbed his air guitar, and started rocking with Tony. Anna and Mo smiled at each other, nodded their heads, and then raced onto the set to join the concert. Within seconds, tech and production crew members, a couple of MBA types in business suits, a woman with blonde hair, and some tattooed, earringed guys hopped onto the set and joined the impromptu rock fest.

After a couple of minutes Tony jumped back up onto the chair, faced the cameras, and mimed the final lyrics. The song abruptly ended, the lights came on, the fog cleared, and the "rockers" on the set immediately stopped rocking; they eyeballed one another, and then broke into laughter.

Tony pumped his fists above his head in triumph, and he dramatically bowed to the rockers around him. Then he turned, faced Luca, and bowed to her. The set immediately became as quiet as a mausoleum.

Luca stared at Tony and then turned to the cameras and, in a deadpan voice, said: "And that, MTV viewers, is my surprise, Mr. Anthony Madison, the Kid in a Bear Suit from Kansas City." She paused, shook her head, and chuckled. "That's it for now. Please stay tuned for my next *MTV News* report." The OFF THE AIR sign flashed on, rock music immediately blasted through the speakers once again, and everyone started rocking—including Luca Stankovic.

"I can't believe we were just on MTV," said Tony.

"Me, either," said Anna. "This place is cool. I want to work here when I grow up."

"So, tell me, Tony, exactly how did you pull that off?" Luca asked as she narrowed her eyes and locked them with Tony's. "You didn't have that much time."

"Well," Tony said, "I hit it off with a production guy when I got here; we talked about this and that, and then before we knew it, it all just sort of fell in pla—"

A phone rang and interrupted Tony. Luca pulled her cell phone out of her pocket. "Yeah, he's here." Pause. "You want to talk to him?" Pause. "Okay, here he is."

Luca handed the phone to Tony. "It's for you."

"Hello," Tony said.

"Hey, kid, this is David Letterman. Was that Luca Stankovic I was on the phone with?"

"Yeah, it was."

"I thought so. She's great, isn't she? As far as I'm concerned, she's the only reason to watch MTV."

"Yeah, she's great."

"Trouble sort of follows you around. Doesn't it, TB?"

"Well, not really, Mr. Letterman."

"That's Dave, kid. And yes it does."

"I heard from Mr. Gore that the three of you were missing. The cops have combed the city looking for you. I was certain that one of New York's giant sewer rats made off with the three of you. And then one of my assistants insisted that I come look at his TV. And do you know what I saw? I saw America's newest hero performing on MTV. You're supposed to be on *my* show, TB, not theirs."

"Yeah, well . . . I'm sorry, Dave. Things just sort of just happen to me."

"That's an understatement, TB."

"Under what?"

"Never mind. I'm going to send my limo over for you. It'll be over in a while. Don't go any-where. Do you understand?"

"Well, Fred Durst, the lead singer from Limp Bizkit, and the rest of his band are here, and they invited us to go to Greenwich Village to get a tat-too with them—you know, Limp Bizkit style."

"I know, TB. I saw them performing with you. No matter what those head-bangers say, you stay put. If you kids get a tattoo, not only will your parents kill the three of you, they'll kill me as well. And besides, Limp Bizkit will be on my show tonight, so you can hang out with them all you want—on my turf."

"If you say so, Dave."

"I say so. And so does Mr. Gore. He's here waiting for you as well."

"Mr. G's there? Good. We were worried about him."

"I think it is the other way around, TB."

"Yeah, you're right, Dave. I'm sure I've driven Mr. G crazy, once again. I bet he was really worried about us."

"Yes, you did and, yes, he was, TB."

"He's sort of like a granny when it comes to worrying. Anyway, can I talk to him?"

"Sure. Here he is."

"Hey, Mr. G, it sure is good to hear your voice."

"I'm not sure I can say the same, TB. Your voice sort of gives me the chills. You're a living nightmare, you know."

"Yeah, I know, Mr. G. Sorry about that."

"You don't know sorry yet, TB. Wait until I get my hands on you."

"Please don't kill me, Mr. G. The airport wasn't my fault. It was Alisha Keenan's fault."

"I don't care whose fault it was, TB. You're still a goner. I've nearly gone crazy worrying about the three of you today."

"Mr. G, I *really* am sorry. We tried to call you several times, but your cell phone didn't work.

We got that stupid no-reception message all the time. We knew you were probably going nuts, so we did try."

"That's *so* responsible of you, TB. I'm *so* impressed that I'm going to nominate you for Kansas City's Citizen of the Year. And since I'm such a nice guy, you're now a half-goner, but only because my cell company stinks."

"Mr. G, you have to believe me. When we couldn't get ahold of you, we decided to find Dave because we knew he'd know how to find you."

"Okay, TB, I believe you—sort of. And as you know, I'm a really sensitive guy, and your story really touches my heart, so your classification has dropped to a quarter-goner. Fortune has come your way, TB. But I'll not negotiate any lower. Is that understood? You still have to answer to me for what happened today."

"Yes, sir. I understand."

"We'll discuss things when you get here, okay?"

"Okay, Mr. G. Please don't kill Anna and Mo. It was all my fault."

"I *never* considered killing them, TB."

"Oh."

"And TB, it . . . uh . . . *is* good to hear your voice."

"Yours, too, Mr. G."

"Okay, enough of this mushy stuff. Mr. Letterman wants to talk to you again. See you in a bit."

"Hey, TB. It's Dave again. I'm not so sure I'd come over here if I were you. Mr. G's a pretty big guy."

"Yeah, but his heart is like a marshmallow, so he probably won't kill me. Well . . . hopefully. Anyway, guess who kissed me, Dave?"

"Who? Madonna?"

"How did you know?"

"Well, TB. I saw her rocking with you during your MTV stint. I ain't blind, you know."

"Whatever, Dave. Anyway, she thinks I'm the cutest thing she's ever seen. She wants to take us to Toys "Я" Us in a couple of minutes and then she wants to take us to—"

"Don't tell her you know me, TB. Or she'll kidnap you. Just stay with Luca when we hang up. No tattoos. No toys. Understand?"

"Yeah."

"Good. Please give the phone back to Luca and let me talk to her. See you soon."

"See you soon, too, Dave," Tony said, handing the phone to Luca.

Luca listened quietly for a couple of minutes and said, "Seriously?" Pause. "My schedule's pretty full, but I'm sure I could squeeze in an afternoon for the *Late Show*." Pause. "I'll get back to you as soon as I can." Pause. "I promise that they won't get out of my sight. And don't bother with sending someone over; I'll personally deliver them to the theater. Why take any chances with them?" Pause. "Of course I'm right. We'll be there after a while. You have my word."

She ended the call and said, "The four of us are going to the Ed Sullivan theater as soon as possib—"

"We'll take 'em," interrupted Mr. Davidsun, nodding at a couple of bikers standing nearby, "and you, as well, Luca. Like you said, why take any chances with 'em?"

"Thanks, Harley. If the Hells Angels can't deliver them to the *Late Show,* then nobody can." Luca paused and looked at the kids. "We're going straight to the lobby. No detours. No toilets. No tattoos. No rock stars. No celebrities. Let's go."

15.
The *Late Show*

Later that day David Letterman sat behind his desk on the set of the *Late Show*. He just finished his top ten list for the evening—The Top Ten Things to Stuff a Turkey With—and the audience roared with laughter.

"Ladies and gentlemen," he interrupted. "Have we got a blockbuster show for you tonight. Arnold Schwarzenegger, Vin Diesel, and Bruce Willis are on the show to tell us about their newest action-packed thriller. Can you believe it? All three of them in the same film!" He paused while the audience hooted and hollered. "And do you like the loud music, kids? Well, you better stick some cotton in your ears because Fred Durst and Limp Bizkit, the bad boy fusionists of hip-hop rock, will be out a little later to trash this joint." He paused again while the audience hooted and hollered some more. "But Schwarzenegger, Diesel, Willis, and Limp Bizkit will have to wait because I've got a hot one for you tonight. It's time to bring out my first guest. You've all seen him on TV and in the papers the last two weeks. Nobody can stop talking about the Kid in the Bear Suit. He stormed the NFL, he's stormed the United States, and he's stormed New York, too. Give a nice round of applause to my replacement when I retire and to America's newest hero, Mr. Anthony TB Madison." He paused, stood up, and looked to the right of the stage as the audience applauded.

But America's newest hero was nowhere to be seen. Tony was not there to make his grand entrance. The applause died out and the Ed Sullivan Theater grew quiet. David Letterman turned to the producer. "Where is he?"

The producer shrugged his shoulders.

David Letterman turned to the audience and shrugged his shoulders, mimicking the producer. "My hotshot producer—who is obviously making *way* too much money—has no idea where the Kid in the Bear Suit is. It seems that for the first time in the history of the *Late Show,* we have lost a guest. This ought to send the ratings into the toilet for us. The black-and-silver-haired chump over at NBC is really going to get some mileage out of this." He looked at the producer again. "You really don't know where he is?"

The producer's head moved back and forth, and he shrugged his shoulders again.

David Letterman stepped in front of his desk and looked at the *Late Show* orchestra director, Paul Shaffer. "Paul, do you know where the kid is?"

"Got me, Dave," Mr. Shaffer said as he ran his hand over his bald head. "I'm in charge of the music, not the guests."

"We've been working together for over twenty years and that's all you come up with? Pretty lame, *eh?*" Mr. Letterman said as he rubbed his chin. "Perhaps you'd rather be in charge of the border crossing between North Dakota and Saskatchewan instead of the music at the *Late Show.*"

"Good idea, Dave," Mr. Shaffer said. "Maybe I'd get to wear one of those cool red uniforms to work every day."

Mr. Letterman rolled his eyes, lowered his chin, and looked over the top of his glasses. "I wonder if Madonna had something to do with—"

The doors to the Ed Sullivan Theater burst open and six Harley-Davidson motorcycles—each with a driver and passenger—roared through, two down the center aisle, two down the left aisle, and two down the right aisle. They stopped at the foot of the stage. The motorcyclists revved their engines, and then, as if on cue, cut them off at the same time.

"Ladies and gentlemen," Mr. Letterman said as he looked at the spectacle before him. "This is worse than the *Invasion of the Body Snatchers*. It's the invasion of Bikers from Hades." He paused and surveyed the bikers. "And I suspect that America's newest hero is the devil behind this invasion."

Tony unwrapped his arms from Mr. Davidsun's belly, slid off his motorcycle, and hopped onto the stage. He confidently walked up to Mr. Letterman and held out his hand. "Hi, Mr. Letterman. I'm Anthony."

"That's Dave to you, and I'm pleased to meet you, too, Anthony, and . . . uh," said Mr. Letterman as he shook hands with Tony and eyeballed the bikers, "where've you been? At a Hell's Angels' cookie bake-off or something?"

"Please call me TB, Dave, and sorry about being late, but . . . as you know, things sort of happen to me."

"An understatement, TB."

"Is that something like *underwear*?" asked Tony.

"I don't have a clue, kid. I figure that if I use big words, I'll impress my boss, and I'll be able to hold on to my job for a while. But that could be a pipe dream when you consider tonight's fiasco, so maybe I better fill out a job application over at Rupert's Deli before I head home tonight," Mr. Letterman said as he walked to the foot of the stage. "So, who are all of these clowns?"

Tony hopped off the stage and gestured for Mo and Anna to join him. "This is Anna and Mo," Tony said as Anna and Mo joined him. "They're my best friends."

Mr. Letterman stepped down into the center aisle and held out his hand. "Glad to meet you, Anna and Mo. You're pretty brave to be TB's best friends, huh?"

"That's an understatement, Mr. Letterman," said Mo as he shook Mr. Letterman's hand.

"I'm happy to meet you, too, Mr. Letterman,"

said Anna as she pumped Mr. Letterman's hand, "and as far as I'm concerned, it's totally understandable why I'm brave enough to be Tony's best friend. Look at him. He's more handsome than Bruce Willis, isn't he?"

"Sorry, Anna, but I plead the Fifth Amendment; Mr. Willis is on the show tonight and he's tougher than me, so I'll keep my trap shut, or I might be visiting an undertaker tomorrow, instead of watching the Weather Channel."

"Your weekends are pretty exciting, huh, Dave?" asked Tony.

"Another understatement, TB," said Mr. Letterman. "After I watch the Weather Channel, I usually organize my socks."

"Like those *cool* white ones you're wearing now?" Tony teased.

"Exactly," said Mr. Letterman, pulling up his pant leg so the cameraman could zoom in for a close shot. "So who are the rest of these characters?"

"The big guy is Mr. Harley Davidsun and the other bikers are members of his band, the Angels," said Tony.

Mr. Letterman and Harley shook hands. "Even geeks in white socks know something good when they hear it, and I have to say, the Angels really rock," said Mr. Letterman. "Harley, I'd love to have the Angels play on my show sometime in the near future. What do you say?"

"It'd be a durn pleasure," drawled Harley.

Tony motioned for two other passengers to join him. A dark-skinned man, decked out in a vivid white turban, and a dark-skinned girl, with long silky black hair, joined Tony. Tony put his arm around the man. "This is Mr. Raj, New York City's best taxi driver and soon to be best child psychologist. He helped us today."

Raj held out his hand. "So, *you* are the letter man! Now I know where to find you." Raj scanned the theater. "Raj on TV now? Maybe my family will see me in Bombay?"

"Yeah, Mr. Raj. You're on TV, but I have no idea if the *Late Show* is shown in Bombay," said Mr. Letterman as he shook Raj's hand, paused, and then looked at the girl. "And who's this young lady?"

Mo stepped forward and smiled at the girl. "This is Divya. She's a friend of Raj's and she's a new friend of mine, uh, *ours*."

Mr. Letterman winked at Mo and placed his hand on Divya's shoulder. "It's a pleasure to have such a pretty young lady on the show."

Divya blushed and said, "It's good to be here."

Tony pointed at the final passenger and smiled. "I think you know who she is."

An attractive woman with blonde hair slid off the last motorcycle and made her way to Mr. Letterman. "Ladies and gentleman, before me stands the *only* reason to watch MTV, Miss Luca Stankovic," said Mr. Letterman as he kissed her on the cheek and took her hand in his. "It's a pleasure to have you on the show, Luca—even under these unfortunate circumstances. How about coming back when things are a bit calmer around here, as we discussed earlier?"

"I watch *you* every chance I get, and I'd love to, Dave," Luca said, smiling at Mr. Letterman, "as long as you promise to wear *black* socks when I'm on the show."

"I promise," said Mr. Letterman as a goofy grin spread across his face, "and I think that maybe I'll ditch the Weather Channel tomorrow and tune into MTV instea—"

"Good plan," interrupted Tony. "And after you watch MTV, why don't you tune into the Fashion Channel and check out this season's designer socks?"

Laughter rippled through the audience.

Mr. Letterman shook his head and smiled. "You're pretty funny, TB. Maybe you'll have your own show someday."

"There's no doubt about it, Dave, because I'm going to take over for you when you retire."

"With the way this episode's going, you might have yourself a job on Monday, TB," said Mr. Letterman, looking at his watch. "But this is *my* show for the next forty minutes, and it's time to move it along."

"If you say so, Dave."

Mr. Letterman looked at the producer. "I say so. And Mr. Paid-Too-Much says it's time for a commercial. All of you *Late Show* lugs—sitting around the stage with what seems to be nothing to do—listen up. When we come back, I want the cycles out of here and the surprise 'guests' seated in the audience . . . and I want America's newest hero seated next to my desk."

A couple of minutes later the motorcycles were gone and Anna, Mo, Raj, Divya, Luca, Mr. Davidsun, and the bikers were seated in the audience. Tony sat in one of two plush chairs next to Mr. Letterman's desk, and Mr. Letterman sat behind his desk.

"Finally, I can say, welcome to the *Late Show,*

TB," said Mr. Letterman, as he looked at his note cards. He tossed the cards over his back and they fluttered into the model of Manhattan, situated behind his desk. "I guess I don't need those anymore. It seems that a certain kid from Kansas City made them irrelevant."

"Irrele—what?" asked Tony.

"It doesn't matter, TB. Let's just say the show isn't going as I planned. So tell me—"

"Dave, where's Mr. G?" interrupted Tony.

"I think he's backstage, in the Green Room, hanging with Schwarzenegger, Diesel, Willis, Durst, and the rest of the slightly insane Limp Bizkit guys. Do you want to see him?"

"Yeah! Believe it or not, I miss him."

"I'm not sure the feeling is reciprocal with him."

"Reciprocal? You can stop using big words, Dave," Tony said as a mischievous smile spread across his face. "You don't have to impress your boss anymore. I'm taking over for you on Monday. Remember?"

Mr. Letterman smiled and rolled his eyes. "The *Late Show with Tony Baloney*. It has possibilities, eh, Paul?"

"It sounds good, Dave," said Mr. Shaffer. "Maybe I won't have to take that job at the border now. TB, will you keep me on the payroll?"

"Sure thing, Mr. Shaffer," said Tony. "As long as you don't wear white geek socks to work."

"I wouldn't be caught dead in the—"

"Ladies and gentlemen," interrupted Mr. Letterman. "I'd like to introduce you to the guy that had the guts to actually bring my replacement to New York City. Let's give a big round of applause to Mr. Tom Gore."

A loud applause rippled through the audience as Mr. Gore walked onto the stage. Mr. Letterman met Mr. Gore beside the second guest chair, whispered something in his ear, and shook his hand. Both men chuckled and then took their seats.

Tony got up and gave Mr. G a hug. "Hey, Mr. G. Good to see you!"

Mr. G gave Tony a half hug and lightly pushed him away. "TB, I'm happy to see you, too. And I'm most happy to see that the three of you weren't arrested by the cops or kidnapped by Madonna or abducted by Limp Bizkit, but let's go easy on the sentimental stuff. Okay? We *are* on national TV.

Remember? I'd hate to tarnish my tough-guy image."

"Sure, Mr. G. I understand," said Tony as he sat down. "What was that whisper about?"

"A quick discussion about whether or not we should chain you to your chair for the rest of the show; a proactive move that could prevent disaster."

"Yeah," added Mr. Letterman. "As I mentioned once before, TB. Trouble sort of follows you around. And I'm already in enough trouble with my boss, so I don't need any more tonight. Okay?"

"Sure thing, Dave," said Tony as he shrugged his shoulders and smiled. "I'm just an innocent kid from Kansas City. What else could happen?"

"I don't even want to consider what other disasters lurk around the corner due to the influence of an innocent kid from Kansas City," said Mr. Letterman, "but what I would like to know is *why*? Why did you send me letters pleading to be invited on the show? Why did you send me hilarious 'top ten' lists? Why did you drive your parents, teacher, and principal crazy in your quest to get me to recognize you? Why were you a major nuisance in New York City today? And why did you bring some Hell's Angels to my show?"

"Because you're the best thing that ever happened to TV, Dave," Tony said sincerely. "And I just had to meet you. I had to be on your show. No matter what."

"Well, you made it," said Mr. Letterman as he removed his glasses and pretended to wipe tears from his cheeks with the back of his hand. Then he got up, stepped around his desk, and tousled Tony's hair. "You've really touched my heart, kid; now I know that I have at least one fan in the world."

"Maybe you have two fans, Dave," said Tony. "Don't forget about a certain someone that works over at MTV."

"Oh, yeah," said Mr. Letterman as sat back down. He paused a second, and a goofy smile spread across his face again. "How could I forget about the *only* reason to watch MTV?"

"Maybe your socks affect your memory or something."

Laughter bounced around the theater.

"Could be, TB. You never know. But one thing I do know is that I've got three *very* famous big guys waiting for me backstage; and if I don't get them on the show tonight, I *won't* be able to fill out a job application at Rupert's Deli, if you know what I mean. So, before I let you go, do you have any last minute surprises for me?"

"Well, Dave, I actually do," said Tony. "Check it out."

A curtain rose on the side of the stage revealing Fred Durst standing beside what looked like a dentist's chair. He held up a small machine and smiled.

"I am not letting him work on my teeth. You know he's slightly insane," said Mr. Letterman.

"I'm not gonna work on your teeth," said Fred as he placed his baseball cap backward on his head, pushed up a sleeve on his T-shirt, and flexed his multi-tattooed arm. "I was a world-class tattoo artist before I became a famous head-banger, Dave. And now I'm gonna give you a tattoo, Limp Bizkit style."

"No way," said Mr. Letterman.

"Yes way," said Tony. "You and I are going to get the first tattoos ever given on the *Late Show*. We'll each get a tattoo that says TLS."

"No way; your parents would kill you *and* me. Anyway, you're just a kid, so you'd need their permission."

Tony took a piece of paper out of his pocket and unfolded it. "Yes way. Here's a fax from my parents. It says I can get a tattoo. Both of them signed it."

Tony handed the paper to Mr. Letterman. Mr. Letterman read it and then handed it to Mr. Gore. Then Mr. Letterman said lamely, "It's a fake fax, right?"

Mr. Gore read the paper and smiled at Tony. He stood up, pulled Tony to a standing position, and said, "You're something else, TB. I've always wanted a tattoo. So let's get one, Limp Bizkit style." He paused and looked at Mr. Letterman. "You coming, Dave?"

Mr. Letterman reluctantly joined Mr. Gore and Tony. "I should have my head examined."

"That's what Mo always says," Tony said as he looked at Fred Durst. "What are we standing here for? Fred's waiting for us; it's time to rock and roll."

Fred laughed (slightly insanely, of course) as he held up his tattoo needle. Then another set of curtains rose behind Fred Durst revealing the rest of Limp Bizkit, complete with instruments and electronic equipment. They immediately launched into a song, and Fred Durst danced like a semi-crazed lunatic as he waved the tattoo needle above his head . . . and Tony, Mr. Gore, and Mr. Letterman walked into *Late Show* history.

Epilogue:
The Announcement

Five hundred restless kids sat in the Riverside Elementary School gymnasium the Monday morning after Thanksgiving break. They were waiting for the start of a special assembly that was being held in honor of one of their fellow students.

Mrs. Hernandez took the stage and stepped behind a microphone. She adjusted the height of the microphone and said, "Welcome to this special assembly. As you may have heard, one of our fifth-grade students was a guest on the *Late Show with David Letterman* last Friday. This is the first time a student from our school has ever appeared on a television show. Even though his methods for reaching his goal were somewhat *unconven-*

tional." She paused, smiled, and looked at Mr. Gore. "He never gave up and he worked hard to reach it, so I thought it appropriate to recognize him for making his dream come true. Boys and girls, please welcome America's newest hero back to Kansas City."

A loud applause exploded through the audience. Kids whistled, hooted, and hollered as Tony walked onto the stage and stood beside Mrs. Hernandez. Mrs. Hernandez raised her hand and signaled silence. The applause died down, and Mrs. Hernandez said, "Tony has a couple of things he wants to say, and then there will be a short question-and-answer session. So, without further ado, let's hear from Anthony Madison, Riverside Elementary's newest celebrity."

Mrs. Hernandez lowered the microphone and left the stage.

Tony cleared his throat, and said, "Being a guest on the *Late Show* was a dream come true for me. It was by far the coolest thing that has ever happened to me. But I never would have made it without the support of some special people. Mom, Dad, and Maria, thanks for being a great family and putting up with me. Anna and Mo, thanks for being the best friends in the world." Tony paused and looked at Mrs. Hernandez as the corners of his lips turned up in a mischievous grin. "Mrs. Hernandez, thanks for not *terminating* me."

"You're welcome, TB," Mrs. Hernandez said from the side of the stage. "But please remember that there are still several months of school left, and my principal instinct tells me that I haven't seen the last of you, so I'm sure there's still plenty of time left for *termination*."

Tony laughed. "You're pretty funny, Mrs. H. You should be on the *Late Show* someday. I'll put in a good word for you with Mr. Letterman."

"And I'll put in a good word for you with the Grim Reaper, and we'll see if we can postpone the Big *T*," said Mrs. Hernandez. "Would you please carry on?"

"Sure," said Tony as he looked at Mr. Gore, seated in the audience with his class. "My final thank-you goes to the best teacher in the world. Mr. G, thanks for believing in me—even though I pretty much drive you crazy. You *really* are the best. And . . . thanks for not *killing* me."

Tony began clapping his hands, and within seconds, the audience joined in with a thunderous applause. When the applause died down, Mr. Gore stood up and said, "Thanks, TB. I'm not sure I'm the best teacher in the world, but I might be the craziest. One has to be slightly of unsound mind to put up with you. And . . . I didn't *kill* you this time, TB. But I make no promises for the future. Regardless, you're . . . uh . . . *unique* and I'm proud of you."

"Thanks, Mr. G! You're a *unique* teacher and you're pretty funny, too," Tony laughed. "And speaking of funny, I'd like to share a top ten list with the kids of Riverside Elementary that Mr. Letterman and I wrote together. I'm going to read it on his show tonight by live satellite feed." Tony paused and pushed a button on a nearby overhead projector, and the following list was projected on a large screen behind him:

THE TOP 10 REASONS I DIDN'T GET MY HOMEWORK DONE

10. I won the lottery and now I'm a millionaire and I don't need to do any stupid homework.
9. I just read an article in the *New England Journal of Medicine* that said that homework is harmful to your health.
8. Homework? Well, you see, technically speaking, I live in a house, so how can I do *homework* without a guilty conscience? Shouldn't it be housework?

7. I went to a ticker-tape parade last night . . . and well. . . .
6. I got hit on the head last night and now I can only read Chinese.
5. My dorky sister·thought it was toilet paper and flushed it away.
4. My mom thought it was dirty underwear and washed it.
3. Uh . . . sorry . . . I thought you said it was due in the year 2050.
2. I was kidnapped by aliens last night, and after they returned me to Earth, I realized that I left my homework on their spaceship.
1. I was a guest on the *Late Show with David Letterman* and I left my homework on his desk.

Tony read the list out loud, and then said, "Mr. Letterman says that whenever you just can't get your homework done . . . or you just don't want to do it . . . or maybe you just plain forget, and you know your teacher is going to kill you the next day when you go to school empty-handed, don't worry because all you need is a good excuse . . . and now you have ten of them!"

The audience burst into wild applause. Tony bowed several times. As the applause ended, Tony bent down and took some things out of a small box on the stage. One by one, he held up a T-shirt, baseball cap, mouse pad, and coffee mug. "These are official *Late Show* things autographed by Mr. Letterman. Mrs. Hernandez is going to organize a raffle sometime later this week and each of you will have a chance to win one of them."

Kids yelled. Kids whistled. Kids jumped up and down. Finally, Mrs. Hernandez stepped in to restore order. She whistled into the microphone and the free-for-all ground to a halt. "That's enough commotion. Please sit down and try to act like semicivilized elementary students," she said as she waited for the students to take their seats. She looked at her watch. "Tony, there's only a few minutes left. You can take a few questions and then this assembly is over because it is almost time for lunch."

A kid in the back of the gymnasium raised his hand.

"Yeah, you, in the back, with the green shirt," said Tony.

"I heard you got a tattoo. Is it true and what did it feel like?"

"Yeah, I got one," Tony said as he raised his pant leg and pushed his sock down, "right here on my ankle. It says TLS. And yeah, it hurt like the opposite of heaven."

"Cool," said the kid in the green shirt.

Next Tony called on a kid on the side of the gymnasium. "The girl with the red hair and pink sweatshirt."

"You sort of caused a lot of trouble around here for the last few months. And I heard that some crazy things happened in New York. My parents would have grounded me for the rest of my life if I had been you. Did your parents kill you or anything?" asked the girl.

"Well . . . my parents came close to killing me a few times, and they were pretty tough on me for some of the things I did, but they are the best parents in the world and they are proud of me because I finally made it to *Late Show*."

Tony called on a kid in the front row. "You, in the Chiefs T-shirt."

"How come David Letterman wears dorky white socks all the time?"

"I've been wondering that myself. Once a geek, always a geek, I guess," said Tony.

Tony called on a kid in the middle of the gymnasium. "The *really* brave kid wearing the Denver Broncos T-shirt."

"Now that you made it to the *Late Show,* what do you plan to do next?" asked the kid.

Tony paused a second, and a sly smile spread across his face. "That's for me to know and the world to find out."